THE MAFIA DON'S CAPTIVE

ROSA MILANO

PROLOGUE

MARCO

I have a suite of rooms ready for when my captive arrives. It's a simple enough system. There's the bedroom. Looks like any other except for the ropes I'll use to keep her bound while I explain the rules to her.

I make a mental note to get fresh bedding put on there before she gets here. She'll have her own ensuite bathroom. Shower cubicle with clear glass doors so I can watch her getting clean after I finish with her.

Next to her bedroom is the punishment room. The red room. So called for the carpet and the color her ass will turn once I've spanked her into submission.

There's the chair with straps to hold her down, a vibrator built into the seat at the front edge. Works well, had it made bespoke back in Italy.

Wooden horse next to it. That's for her to be tied along or draped over depending on what mood takes me. More straps on the wall for if I want to tie her up there instead.

I pull open one drawer. Butt plugs of a variety of sizes and shapes. Next drawer contains paddles and leather belts.

Below that are bottles of lube and rows of vibrators. Gags, blindfolds, handcuffs. Everything a man like me needs to make sure she knows her place.

She might think she'll be able to leave but she's wrong. This is going to be for the rest of her life. She will never leave my house again. Even if she escaped the building, we're on an island in the middle of the ocean. Where's she going to run to?

I close the drawers and head through to the third room, my personal favorite. This is where pleasure meets pain. It's the main bathroom. An examination table with leg stirrups to make shaving easier. Clawfoot bath, big enough for two. I'll enjoy the sight of her soaking in there soon enough. My cock twitches at the thought.

The last room along this corridor is the one she'll have to work hard to see inside. We'll see whether she gets to go in there. That's my bedroom. One day soon, she'll stop being so afraid of me, start begging to be allowed to spend the night in my arms. They always do.

I spend the rest of the day waiting. I know she'll ring me as soon as she gets my message. By the evening I've had enough of waiting. I'm a patient man, but I have my limits. If she's not even willing to discuss appropriate punishment for her crimes, I'm going to have to take steps to bring her here myself.

I sail my boat across to the mainland, leaving instructions for Ben and Horace to keep a close eye out in case she arrives under her own steam. I doubt she will. I suspect she's hiding out at her place, hoping I'm bluffing, praying I'll leave her alone. She'll soon see I haven't forgotten her. How could I? She's my obsession.

I get to the mainland and dock my boat, heading for the long stay parking garage. The Bentley isn't where I left it,

"By the time I got back on my feet he was gone and so was the money."

"You really screwed up, Ellie. I can't believe I trusted you with this."

"I told you I didn't want to do it."

"And I told you what would happen if you didn't."

I've still got the bruises from last time I refused to do something for her and Sergio. She smiles out of nowhere and it's creepy. She never smiles at me. "Lucky for you, we've a way for you to fix things."

"How?" I ask with a sinking feeling in the pit of my stomach.

I feel someone looking at me. I try to ignore it. I can't help but look.

There he is. The man they're all fawning over. He's staring right at me from his table, ignoring his server. I feel myself shrinking under his gaze. Even from across the room it's like he's trying to strip me. I tug at the straps of my dress, feeling overexposed all of a sudden. It doesn't help that Sergio is still staring at my tits. "I have a face," I tell him, waving my arms in front of him.

"See that guy over there," she says, pointing behind me. "The one who's been staring at your ass the entire time you've been whining at me?"

I turn and there he is. The brute with the five thousand dollar suit. He's walking over to the bar. A politician I vaguely recognize is approaching him, hand outstretched. The guy just looks down at the hand until it withdraws. The politician tries slapping him on the shoulder and immediately regrets his mistake.

I feel scared on that guy's behalf. I can't imagine what it would be like to be on the receiving end of that tall man's anger. His voice is inaudible, like he's whispering but it's clear the politician is scared of what he hears. He's nodding too fast, his face white, his brow a sheen of sweat.

A hand waves in front of my face, and I turn my attention back to my sister. She's grinning coldly at me. "Earth to Ellie. We've a job for you to make up for your fuck up."

My heart sinks. "Please, Chrissie. I told you, if I get caught again, I'm going to prison this time."

"So don't get caught. Come on, it's an easy enough lift. It's this or you can explain to the Don how you lost his money. I hear he skins people who cost him money. That what you want? Or do you want to do one more job for me before you go off to college?"

I shudder. "What's the job?"

"See that man there. That is Esposito's only living rival. Marco Alessi. Don of the Alessi famiglia."

"I see him."

"His keys. Always keeps them in his right pants pocket. Got a Bentley outside that's worth a lot more than the money you lost tonight. You get the keys and we take the car to Esposito. Everyone's happy."

Her boyfriend is looking at me funny. "What?" I ask him. "You got a problem with me?"

He turns to Christine, whispering in her ear again.

She nods. "He doesn't think you're good enough to dip Marco's keys. Want to tell him how many times you've done this before?"

Too many is the answer. So often Christine has needed money, and I've been the one to get it for her. I don't remember my life being any different.

She kisses Sergio on the forehead. "Don't worry. She's been doing this since she was a little kid. Made us a lot of dough, haven't you, sis?"

"What if she gets caught?" Sergio asks in a thick Italian accent.

"She won't."

I glance at my target. He's got his whiskey but he seems in no rush to go back to his table. He's leaning back on the bar and watching me with an intensity so strong I'm surprised smoke isn't rising from my dress. I mustn't be intimidated by him. Just another mark. One more job. Make up for getting mugged.

I get a feeling this is going to go wrong. I look at Christine but she's shoving me up on my feet. "How else do you intend to pay off your debt?" she asks. "You got any cash in that cobwebbed coochie of yours?"

Sergio laughs and I want to hit them both. Rage boils up in me. It's not fair. Why do I have to do it? All I want is to go straight, stop stealing things. But I live in Christine's place and she won't hesitate to throw me on the streets if I don't do what she says.

I get to my feet and do the tipsy walk, making it look like I'm buzzed but not hammered. I wobble slightly from side to side as I approach the bar. He's watching me approach.

This close he doesn't just look good. He looks smoking hot. Dangerous too. What are those tattoos on his knuckles? How'd he get that scar on his left cheek?

I get the funny feeling he knows what I'm about to do. He's looking right at me and then his eyes move down my body. That's when I know it'll be all right. He's just like all the other men. Too interested in my tits to see where my hands are going.

I trip and fall at the exact right moment. He sticks his arms out to catch me and in a second it's done. My hand dips into his pocket and then the keys are bunched in my fist. Didn't make a sound. Then I'm standing up, mumbling an apology, touching his chest, using my eyes, blinking slowly, flirting like crazy. His chest feels like solid rock. I turn at once to walk away.

He catches my wrist. "That was foolish," he says, not letting go. His voice is a deep rumble, a hint of Italian to it. "What's your name?"

"Catherine," I say, giving him the first name that comes into my head.

"Your real name."

"That is my real name."

"Don't bullshit a bullshitter. Give me your name and I let go of you."

"My name's Catherine Albertson."

"So you want to play games? Fine. Come with me." He pulls me through the crowd at the bar.

I protest but not too loudly. I don't want attention on me from anyone else until I've handed over the keys.

He pushes open a door and then we're standing in the kitchen. Around us the staff are yelling at each other. The heat is overwhelming. "I don't think we're supposed to be back here," I tell him.

He smiles but there's no warmth to it. "I doubt they'll mind. I just bought the restaurant." He continues dragging me through the kitchen and then through another door. Finally he lets go of me.

"You could have broken it," I tell him, rubbing where he grabbed me. My eyes scan the room. I'm in an office with a frosted glass window at the back. Too small to escape through. No, maybe not. I might just be able to do it. The perks of being five foot three and never getting enough to eat.

"You did a bad thing," he says, turning the lock of the office door. "Didn't you, Cat?"

"I don't know what you're talking about. I only tripped into you."

He reaches out with his hand open. "Give them back."

"Give what back. I don't know what you're talking about."

"Does Esposito think I will fall for such amateur tactics? Tell him from me, I am not giving him the painting."

His hand is still outstretched. I can feel the keys hidden in my fist. They feel much heavier than they did before.

He's standing between me and freedom. The only option is to try to run for the window. If it's locked, I'm screwed.

It might be open. I twist my head, trying to make it look natural. "I've no idea what you're talking about," I say as I glance at the window latch. Looks unlocked to me.

"I will give you one chance to tell me the truth. Who told you to take my keys? Esposito? You tell him from me, he can come see me himself if he wants to discuss this. Not send some honeypot to distract me with her juicy tits and her tight little pussy while she takes my keys from my pocket. I've a good mind to spank you for what you've done but I don't think I'd be able to resist fucking that fine ass of yours while I'm at it."

"Listen, I think you've got the wrong impression. I don't know any Esposito. I just fell over, that's all."

"So if I open your hand, I won't find my car keys bunched up there? Tell me the truth, Cat, and maybe I'll let you walk out of here without a spanking."

TWO

ELLIE

I glare up at him, trying not to be afraid. "You can't keep me here, you know that, right? This is kidnapping. I'm going to call the police right now."

"How? You left your handbag at your table when you came to steal my car keys. Does he think I keep the painting in the car? Tell him from me, he will never find it."

My heart sinks as I realize he's right. I turn and dart for the window. I get it open and I'm halfway out but I get no further. He grabs hold of my ankle and drags me back into the room.

"Help!" I scream but it's the only word I get out. An instant later there's a gag around my mouth. I don't even know where it's come from. He looms over me, grabbing my flailing wrists as I try to lash out at him. He wraps a cord around them, pulling it tight, knotting it in place before stepping back from me. "I warned you," he says. "I only give a chance and you just lost it."

He leans out the window, scooping up the keys I just

dropped out there. "Still going to pretend you didn't take them?" he asks, waving them in my face.

While he's talking I run for the door and try to pull it open. I get my hands on the lock but before I can turn it he's yanking me off my feet, lifting me into his arms. I kick out at him but he snarls at me.

"Enough!" he says in a voice so deep it sends shudders through my whole body. "You are acting like a spoilt brat." He sets me back on my feet. "Spoilt brats get their hides tanned. Do not move!" he says, pointing a finger at me. "You move and you will not leave this room alive. Esposito clearly thinks I am a fool if you are the best he can send after me. I will send you back to him in pieces if you don't behave."

He steps back, nodding as I glare at him. I can taste the cloth of the gag in my mouth. I get the horrible feeling he means what he says. Is he going to spank me or kill me?

"You have no idea who I am, do you?" he asks, taking off his jacket and draping it over the chair behind the desk. "I can tell by your face. You have no idea who you're foolishly trying to steal from. No matter. You'll learn." As he walks back around, he's uncuffing his sleeves, rolling them up above his elbows. The muscles in his arms are huge.

"You stole from me," he continues. "I always punish those who steal from me. Bend over the desk."

I look back at him and shake my head. There's no way that's happening. I go for the door again but he grabs me with a growl, holding me tight against him, whispering into my face.

"Bend over willingly or I bend you over myself." I shake my head again. "So be it," he adds, grabbing my shoulders and spinning me around, shoving me down over the desk.

He presses his palm into the small of my back and no

matter what I try to do, I'm going nowhere until he loosens his grip. I'm pinned in place, unable to get away.

He takes hold of the hem of my dress and lifts it to my hips. I try to wriggle free again but he keeps his palm in place. With one foot he kicks my ankles apart.

"Do you know what's going to happen now?" he asks, the fingers of his free hand curling into the waistband of my panties. The feel of his rough skin on my ass reaches through my fear, sending heat spreading deep through me. It's heat that I don't want. He mashes my buttocks in his fist, tugging it to the side. "That cherry looks like it hasn't been plucked," he says, stroking over my asshole. "Maybe I should just fuck it. Show you what happens when you lie to me."

"Let me go," I try to say but the only sound that gets through the gag is a muffled nothing.

"I'm going to teach you a lesson," he continues, ripping my panties off in one movement. The sound of fabric tearing sends my pulse through the roof.

"Please," I try to say but the gag works too well to make myself understood.

He leans down, his face close to mine, his hand back on my ass, working low, almost touching my pussy. "I'm going to spank you for being such a bad girl," he says, lifting a hand into the air. He brings it down onto my ass an instant later, still staring into my eyes.

The sting whips through me. A burning sensation spreads from my buttocks to somewhere deeper inside me. I feel my clit come to life. I'm furious with him for the effect he's having on me. I don't want this.

I'm terrified of him but there's another feeling, one that I don't like. One that's edging forward to the tips of my consciousness. When he spanks me a second time it bursts out, shouting in my head.

You like the pain.

I don't. I don't like this. I don't want his enormous palm slapping down on my ass a third time. I don't want to be held in place by his powerful hand. Most of all, I don't want him to look between my legs because, if he does, he'll see how wet I've become.

He spanks me again, this time lower down. I cry out into the gag and try to shift in place. His hand remains on my ass, invading the valley between my buttocks, running down over the little hole that's hidden there. I fight a sudden desire to push back against his finger. What the hell is wrong with me?

He moves his hand lower, stroking over my pussy. "Soaking wet," he says with a chuckle so deep it sounds like a truck rolling by on the freeway. "So you do like being punished. I knew it. I knew from the instant I saw you that you would like this. You want me in you, don't you, Cat? You want me to fuck that ass of yours."

He brushes over my clit and I have to clamp down on the moan that's trying to escape me.

His finger continues to circle my clit. "You like this, don't you? You like the pain?"

I don't respond. I can't do anything. I'm too lost in the intensity of the feeling between my legs. Where he spanked me every nerve ending is on fire. He strokes around my asshole again and I can't resist pushing back onto him.

He chuckles once again. "So eager," he says. "I bet I can make you come with no effort at all."

His hand is between my legs again. His thumb slides into my pussy, stretching me wide while his fingers slide back and forth over my clit. He leans down and whispers in my ear, his hot breath making my skin tingle. "Come for me,

Cat. Come for me right now. Show me you can be a good girl, not just a spoiled brat and an amateur thief."

I groan into the gag, my legs giving way. I don't want to climax. I don't want to be here. I don't want to have my panties torn in pieces and my dress up over my waist. I want to get the hell out of this place. I don't want to want him this much.

I can't help myself. His touch is insanely intense. The heat grows overwhelming. He speeds up his movements, pressing his hips against mine. I can feel the bulge of his cock through his pants and the thought of it sliding into me is enough to tip me over the edge.

A climax races through me, making me cry out at the sheer overwhelming bliss rocking my body. My knees give way and my pussy grips around his finger, wanting so much more. Even my ass feels empty, like it wants him in there at the same time.

I'm still recovering when he pulls my panties back up and spins me around to face him. I push my dress back down into place as he steps back and stares at me. His eyes are flashing with hunger and when I glance down I see one hell of a tent in his pants. What size cock can make a bulge like that?

"So you can obey me," he says. "That's good to know. Such a shame I have business to attend to this evening." He unlocks the door without taking his eyes off me. "If we ever meet again, my little Cat, I'm going to keep you for good."

He pulls open the door, putting a finger to his right ear as if he's listening to someone. "Apparently, your friends have already left in a cab. They have taken your handbag with them." He reaches over the desk to his jacket and I get a look at his firm looking ass. Does he have to look so fine?

He turns around with his wallet in his hand and pulls

out a thick wad of banknotes. "Here," he says, holding out at least five hundred dollars. "For your ride home." He reaches out and unties my hands.

As soon as they're free, I pull the gag away from my mouth. "You sick fuck," I spit at him. "Who the hell do you think you are?"

"I'm Marco Alessi and you're a poor thief who got caught," he replies. "A rank amateur criminal who got punished for her crimes. Would you rather the police were told of your indiscretion?"

I look down at the floor. I'm not going to prison.

"I thought not. We handled things in private and the matter is now concluded. Run along, little Cat, before I change my mind."

"Think you can buy me off like a hooker? Fuck you." I snatch the money from him and toss it into the air. "I'm calling the police on you. You kept me hostage. You abused me. You beat me."

"I punished you for your crime. That is all."

"You...you made me come."

"Did you not enjoy your orgasm, Cat?"

I get a flashback of the moment it hit me. For an instant, I can't say anything. I shake my head. "You got an arrogant answer for everything you smug son of a bitch."

"You enjoyed it but you cannot admit it." He wags a finger at me. "Next time I see you, I will keep you. Be warned."

"Go to hell."

I sprint out of the office without looking back. I crash through the kitchen and out into the restaurant, my ass still stinging from where he spanked me. I march outside and promptly burst into tears. I think about calling the police but it would mean breaking my one unbreakable rule. Never involve the cops. Ever.

I scurry down the street and make a new rule to add to that one. Never involve the cops and go nowhere near Marco Alessi ever again.

THREE

ELLIE

One year later...

I'm in the library when Marco Alessi pops back into my head out of nowhere.

I blame the building. I don't know about you but there's something about libraries that gets my mind racing. Maybe it's because the place is so still and quiet and naughty stuff is the last thing you should think about doing here. Maybe it's just because I'm screwed up. Have been ever since that night.

Christine hasn't spoken to me since. I got arrested the same night for the gambling ring. They said in court I was running the whole thing. No one believed me that I was only there to collect some money. There I was on CCTV, standing in the middle of the room. It wasn't hard to convince the jury I was in charge. So I got eight months, reduced because of my age.

I've tried to contact Christine since I got out but she just told me I was dead to her. So I've had to learn to survive on my own. In so many ways, my life has gotten harder since that night I met Marco Alessi.

I can't help but blame him for it. So why the hell does he come back into my head tonight?

I often think pretty racy things when I'm studying. The higher the floor, the worse it gets. Tonight I'm sitting on the top floor and there's no one here but me.

I'm looking down at my book but I've read the same paragraph four times. Heathcliff is yelling at Cathy but I'm not listening.

All I can think is about is Marco. He's invaded my head, sliding my panties down, leaning me over the desk, not caring who might see us.

It doesn't help that I haven't had a man since that night with him.

Who could hope to match the intensity of that night? The answer is no one. Not a single person my age could do what he did. The way he reached into my soul, bypassed every inhibition and doubt I might have and cut straight to what I needed most. To submit to him, willingly or not.

We didn't even do that much. That's the most screwed up thing about all of this. He dragged me into the office. I had no say in the matter. He bent me over the desk and he spanked me. He whupped my ass with his hand. Then he made me come using the same hand. It was an orgasm like none I've ever had. The ones I give myself don't even come close.

Nothing could ever live up to that night. I've done my best to forget it and him but sometimes he just appears in my mind, normally when my guard's down.

Anyway, I'm in the library and I'm trying my best to study but out of nowhere I think of him. He pops into my head quite a lot, like he lives in there. Tells me he's going to fuck me in the ass right here over this desk, not giving a shit who comes walking this way.

I try to stop him, tell him we can't. It's too public. We'll get in trouble. I'll get banned and then I really am screwed and not in a good way. He doesn't listen. Tells me it's happening. My body is already reacting, heating up as he holds me in place, yanking up the back of my skirt...

"Are you all right?"

I look up and Mrs. Henry is peering down at me over her horn-rimmed glasses. Her eyes are full of concern. "You look a little flushed," she says. "It is warm in here this evening. Want me to open the window."

"No," I say, gathering up my books. "I'm fine. Should be heading home anyway."

"Friday night," she says with a wink. "You getting up to anything exciting?"

"Does a tub of cookie dough ice cream and re-watching Breaking Bad count?"

"You're nineteen, Ellie. You should be out there going crazy. Getting into trouble."

"I'm getting too old for that." I think about the prison sentence and grimace. I'm not getting into trouble anymore. Never again.

"You're a good girl," she says with a sigh. "A bit too good sometimes."

I smile and collect my things. She has no idea about my past. No one has. It's the past. It's gone.

I've moved on. Got a place in a shitty apartment block. It's not a penthouse but at least it's a roof over my head. All I can afford. Better than I've had it in the past. Better than being on the streets.

One day I'll be able to afford my own computer and finish this correspondence course at home. Until then, the library has saved my ass more than once. If I could just stop thinking about Marco when I'm meant to be studying, life would be all right.

Maybe there should be cold showers in libraries. That might help.

I've a vibrator at home. That's a more realistic option. I could bring it with me in my handbag. Scratch that itch next time when it arises.

The thought of it turns my cheeks bright red. I'm glad of the cool night air when I get outside.

The walk to my place isn't too long but it's long enough to bump into two real pieces of shit on the corner by Don's gas station. They're often standing there like a shitty Jay and Silent Bob. I don't know their names. I call them Craterface and Greasyhair. I'm sure you can work out why.

Normally they yell shit at me about my tits and then carry on yakking, but twice they've tried to touch me up. I just walk on by fast as I can. What else can I do? The police wouldn't be interested, even if I was willing to break my rule and call them. Ex-con whining. That's all they'd say.

I don't know what it is about tonight, maybe they've had more to drink than normal. Maybe they're just feeling cocky. Either way they step right out in front of me on the corner. "Where are you going?" Craterface asks. "We're celebrating. Got made associates. You should join us."

"With all those books too," Greasyhair adds. "What are you? Some kind of egghead?"

I go to step around them as they snigger at their superb joke.

They move too, blocking my way. "Want to keep us company?" Greasyhair continues, grinning stupidly at me. "We're a lot more interesting than books. Wuthering Heights? What the fuck's that? Some kind of queer book?"

"Out of my way," I say, trying again to get around them. I want a guardian angel right about now, one with a fantastic left hook.

"Maybe we don't want to get out of your way," Crater-face says. "Maybe we want you to stop looking down your fucking nose at us. We know you've been inside. You ain't no better than us."

"Not that it's any of your business but no I haven't."

"Sure you have. Our new boss told us all about you. You ain't the good girl you pretend to be, Ellie. You should come work for him. He pays well. Bet you looking to sell that ass of yours, aren't you? Make some real cash? Better than being an ex-con with no future. You lez up while you were in there, didya?"

"Bet you did," his friend adds, sniggering. "Bet you fucked the warden too."

"I don't know what you're talking about. I'm just a student. Please, leave me alone."

A car turns into the gas station. They glance that way and I use the distraction to run. I don't slow down until I can't hear their yelling anymore.

I'm going to have to change my route home from now on. I don't like the idea of those two getting any friendlier than they are already. And how did they find out about prison? I don't like that information being out there, not one bit. I'm trying to reinvent myself, become a law-abiding citizen.

I don't encounter anyone else on the way home but I'm still tense when I get in. I put my books down on the counter and then squeeze into the tiny kitchen.

I haven't even boiled the kettle before my cellphone rings. I look at the screen. It's my sister. I haven't heard from her since I got out. I can't believe she's calling me. It better not be another job. Her last one got me eight months.

"Ellie," my sister's voice says when I answer. "I need your help." She sounds worried.

Chrissie?" I say. "What's wrong?"

FOUR

ELLIE

There's a rustling down the line. Then a man's voice comes on. A creepy, oily, voice. Italian accent. Not Sergio, someone else. "You love your sister, Eleanor?"

"What? Who is this?"

"I asked you a question. Do you love your sister?"

"Put Christine back on the phone."

"If you love her, you'll do a job for me."

"What the fuck are you talking about?"

"I have a job that needs doing. You stole money from me. You are also an excellent cat burglar or so I am told. You do this job for me and I write off you and your sister's debt. You turn me down, I take her to one of my brothels to take as many cocks as she can before she gets too old and then she gets her brains blown out. I will give you ten seconds to decide what her fate is to be."

The time ticks down. My mind is whirling. She's in debt. She's been in debt before but this is clearly bad. The guy is serious. I can tell by his voice. I don't want to be a criminal anymore. She told me she hated me, that I was dead to her. The judge said if I come up before him again, it won't be six months. It'll be a lot of years. Gave me one last chance to prove I could stay away from a life of crime.

"What do you say?" the voice asks. "Going to help her?"

She's the only family I've got. "What's the job?"

He laughs down the line. "It's simple enough. I have a crew ready to go who will do the grunt work. They will ferry you to an island. On that island is a house. Inside the house is a study. Inside the study is a painting called *Girl in Chair*. You will bring me that painting and in return I will write off all the debt and, because I'm generous, in addition I will give you ten thousand dollars."

I've never earned that much from one job. I've never earned that much from a hundred jobs. I could get a decent place. I could get a computer. Go to actual college. I could do so much with that money.

He's still talking. "Ten thousand for one night's work. Your sister tells me you're the best. Want to prove it?"

I can't help but feel a spark of pride. I swallow it down. Let that wash over me and I'll be back in the game before I can stop myself. "Why me?"

"I need someone small who understands alarms. Someone who can fit through a narrow window. I also need someone motivated enough to bring the painting to me and not sell it themselves."

"How much is it worth?"

"Not a lot but it has...sentimental value to me. It was stolen from my home by Marco Alessi long ago and I've only just found out where it is being kept thanks to a new colleague of mine. Finally crossed over to the winning team."

"How big are we talking? How heavy?"

"Only one foot square, oil on canvas in a wooden frame. You could carry it under your arm. What do you say? Do you love your sister enough to do this for her?"

I think about some of the shitty things she's done to me over the years. But then I think about the times when I was little and starving and she made sure we always had food to eat. As long as I stole it. "I'll do it."

"Excellent. The crew will wait for you at dock nine in Gordon's Cove at midnight. You will be home by sunrise. Call me on this number when the job's done."

He hangs up. I look down at the phone. I don't even know his name. I try my sister's phone but of course it's turned off. I walk through to the tiny lounge. I sit on the couch and stare at the wall, thinking hard.

It's just one job. Stealing a painting from a house. One job to save her. Do it right and I won't get near a judge. No one will know. I'll be home by sunrise. It's a couple of hours out of my life. I do it or she gets trafficked.

I know he means it. I know the type of people she's owed money to in the past. Sergio hasn't minded borrowing from her to fund his gambling. Got her into horses. Got her into debt on his behalf. Kept her borrowing more. Two hundred vig a week and I had to go out to get it. That was four years ago. Who knows how much she owes now.

What she needs is to get away from that piece of trash but she's her own person. Older than me. Got to let her make her own decisions in life.

I can make mine too. I don't have to help her. I could refuse. I've gone straight.

No, I can't refuse. She's family. The only family I have. I look at the time. Just after eight. That gives me a few hours to get out ready.

It's been a while. I only hope I haven't forgotten how to do this.

I take a shower and tie my hair back when I'm done. I don't want it in my face causing problems. I get dressed in black, hood on ready to go up. Black sneakers that have been my faithful friends on many jobs. They're whisper quiet.

There's a lot of things I don't like about this. I have no preparation time. I don't know the layout of the building, what room the painting's in. How many people are at home. I don't even know what the painting looks like. I can only hope the boat crew can fill me in on some of the details on the way.

Gordon's Cove is a couple of hours away. I get a cab at half nine, using the last of my cash to pay for it. One positive, I'll have plenty of cash come tomorrow morning. Enough to get my own computer. Maybe even enough to move somewhere less shitty. Become a teacher. Give something back to the world. Main thing is my sister will be safe.

I'm silent during the journey. We get there and I pay up, then walk onto the docks. They're quiet. Not surprising at this time of night. If I saw Batman beating up some sleazy looking goons I wouldn't be surprised. This is real life so I see nothing until I get to dock nine.

The boat moored there looks like it's rigged for fishing but I don't see any rods on board. What I do see are three guys and my heart sinks when I look closer. I recognize one of them. "Sister in law," Sergio says when he sees me. "How you doing, Ellie?"

"What are you doing here?" I ask as I get nearer. "Do you know about Christine?"

He doesn't seem that upset, but he does knock his smile off. "Uh-huh. Don't worry though. Don Esposito keeps his word. Get him the painting and he'll let her go without a scratch on her."

"Don Esposito? Where do I know that name from? Don...Don...Don."

"Don means father. His real name's Lorenzo. Mafia, baby. Talking big time crook. He's head of the Esposito family. My famiglia."

"What does he want with Christine?"

"We had a dead cert that took a fall at the first fucking fence," he replies, spitting into the water. "Lost a fortune. Owe him big. Don't worry. He's mob, but he's a straight up guy."

"I somehow doubt that."

He's frowning at me. "What're you saying? You don't think he's a good guy? Know something I don't?"

"I know you don't become Don of a mob family by being a good guy."

"Yeah, well don't worry about that. Worry about the job. Let me introduce you to the crew of the Bellsprit. That brick shithouse over there's Benito and that scrawny motherfucker next to him is Arlo. Say hello, boys."

The other two men grunt my way. Benito is tall and thickset. He's slicked back his hair to cover a bald spot and I can tell from this distance he smells bad. Arlo is shorter and thinner and his eyes never meet mine. They always look either side of me like he's a rabbit expecting a hawk to scoop him up any moment. Sergio's looking as greasy as ever. Greasy hair, skin, smile. The works.

"What do you know about the place?" I ask as he walks up the gangplank onto the boat.

"Big fucking house," he replies. "Huge. Study's in the middle of the building, one window overlooking a courtyard. Another window above the door into the corridor.

Painting's on the wall behind the desk. Door's kept locked but the window above it is about yay big." He holds his hands a foot apart. "Just the right size for someone petite with a tight little ass to squeeze through." The two other men snigger behind me. "Benito will sweep the place for any guards. Arlo will disable the cameras."

"What's your job?"

"Keeping you alive long enough to get the painting."

"So you just need me to get through the study window?"

"And disable the alarm when you take the painting down. The frame's connected to the security system."

"What kind of system?"

"Artex 3000."

I think back to the Artex brand, the layout of the wiring in the control panel, the quickest way of disabling it. Scary how fast it all comes back.

"What happens when I get the painting?"

"We get the fuck out of there before we get caught." He slaps me on the back. "Don't worry. By tomorrow morning, you'll have your sister back and everyone'll be happy. Maybe we have a threeway to celebrate?"

The other men laugh as he starts the engine. With a foul smelling cloud of diesel rising in the wind, we move away from the dock. I get a sinking feeling in my stomach. Something is going to go wrong. I don't know what. All I know is I have a very bad feeling about all this.

FIVE

ELLIE

We're on the water for an hour before the weather starts to turn. At first the night was clear enough but one by one the stars are disappearing over our heads.

"How far is it?" I ask, looking out at the blackness that cloaks us in every direction. The wind's picking up and the boat's lurching from side to side. Not a good sign.

"Another hour or so," Sergio says. "It's not that far from the coast but we can't approach direct. Got to look like we're a set of lost fishermen. Might be radar. Who knows what shit he's got protecting the place."

The sea gets choppier. The boat rises and falls and I start to feel nauseous. I'm not used to rough seas, and it seems neither is Sergio. As the weather grows worse he starts to struggle with the steering. A couple of times I could swear we're turned around the wrong way, but he just keeps snapping that he knows what I'm doing.

I look at the back of his head and wonder what Christine sees in him. He's nothing special as far as I can tell.

Not that I'm one to talk. She's at least capable of holding down a long-term relationship. Getting engaged even. One day I might be watching her walking down the aisle with him. A family next.

What have I got? A vibrator and a yearning for a guy who spanked me once a year ago. Didn't even screw and I'm still obsessing over him. Never saw him again though.

I made some discreet enquiries, but I came up against one wall after another. Some people said he'd gone to Europe. A couple of guys swore he was dead. Someone inside said he'd changed his name and moved to Montana.

"Marco Alessi," I say to Sergio.

"What about him?"

"Any idea where he ended up?"

"Yep," he replies. "Nearly got whacked after the bank thing so made himself disappear."

"What bank thing?"

"You didn't hear about it? I thought everyone knew about it."

"Not me."

He glances my way. "Fucking piece of shit whacked two random kids and Don Esposito's nephew in the same night. Supposed to be a simple bank job, but he killed Elda and took the money for himself. The Don put a hit out on him and he vanished same night. Doesn't take a genius to work out what happened. He's hiding with the money, earning interest, feet up, blood dripping off his hands. No wonder Esposito wants the painting. It'll bring him out of hiding to get it back."

"Wait, it's Marco Alessi's painting?"

"Didn't we tell you?"

"No, no, you did not."

"Well, I have now. Don't worry. From what I hear, he's

gone full Howard Hughes. Hiding out in his mansion, growing his nails long and never leaving his bedroom. Got a couple of servants bringing him food and that's it. Ben and Horace. Ben's the cook and Horace is an old coot who cleans as much as he bitches. We'll be in and out. Marco's out of the game. Lost it entirely."

"I don't know," Benito yells from the back of the boat, his voice almost lost in the growing wind. "Alessi family are still in business in the city. Someone's got to be running the show while he's hiding out."

"Poletti," Arlo says. "He's taken over."

"Who's Poletti?" I ask.

"Alessi's consigliere. He's running things while Marco's gone."

"Bullshit," Benito adds. "Where'd you hear that?"

"Saw it with my own eyes. Poletti was at the track just last week when me and Sergio were there, talking to his capos and he didn't look like he was there to bet on the nags."

We hit a gigantic wave and I'm almost knocked off my feet. "Put your lifejackets on," Sergio yells. "I got a bad feeling about this storm."

Benito rummages in a chest that's welded to the stern. "Why'd he have to pick tonight to do it?" he asks no one in particular.

Sergio yells back at him. "Because the storm matches our cover story, you dipshit."

Inside the chest are life jackets. Benito passes one to me and I slip into it just as the rain starts to fall. It's a real cloudburst and it hurts when the deluge hits me. I pull my hood up but it soaks through immediately. I blink away what I can. Sergio is spinning the wheel and the boat's rocking even more, creaking under our feet.

"How far?" Arlo shouts.

Sergio looks at something on his cellphone. "Not far. Should see the lights soon. Over there somewhere."

I squint where he's pointing but I can't see anything. The rain feels like it's hitting me from the horizon rather than the sky. The boat lifts and falls and spray splashes over the side, sloshing around at my feet. "Get bailing," Sergio shouts.

A bucket is shoved in my hand and I scoop up as much seawater as I can, tossing it over the side, not easy with the life jacket's bulk getting in the way.

There's another wave and I start to lose my balance. I tip forward and catch my arm on the side of the boat. I think I'm safe but then the wind blows me suddenly to the left.

As I go that way, we hit something in the water. There's a crunch and a jolt and then I'm flying through the air. I scream but the sound is lost in the gale.

I hit the water and sink straight under the foaming surface. The cold hits me an instant later and my mouth opens to gasp. I'm still under and I don't breathe air. All I get is salt water filling my lungs. It's freezing cold and I'm sure I'm going to drown.

I bounce up to the surface, and I start to panic, spluttering as I duck down again. The life jacket starts to work, bringing me back up. This time I stay up. I yell for help but the noise is nothing compared to the storm. I can see the boat and it's turning, a light sweeping the water. I wave and shout but they're looking in the wrong place.

I feel my heart sinking as I see it moving away whenever my waves get high enough. They're still looking in the wrong place. They're moving further away and then a wave rises in front of my face, washing me in the opposite direction. I

THE MAFIA DON'S CAPTIVE

can't see anything but spray for a moment but then I'm back down and I can see them. They're further away. I try to yell again but I just get another mouthful of water when I try.

That's when I know I'm going to drown. The feeling hits me with absolute certainty. It's a strangely calm feeling. Panic leaves me and the absolute certainty of it takes away all remaining emotions. Part of me wants to tear off the life jacket, stop the interminable waiting.

I'm drifting on my back and I don't know where I am or where I'm heading. All I know is that I'm going to die out here. I want to cry but nothing comes.

I'll never see my sister again. Never find out what happens to her.

I get a flash of my life and it feels like such a huge fucking waste. Parents that died before I can even remember them. Foster parents that were scum of the earth. Sneaking out with my sister carrying me and not looking back. Living on the streets. Almost starving. Freezing every winter. The only warm place to hide was the library. Learning to read with the help of the librarian.

She was a retired teacher. Can't even remember her name now. Me and Chrissie all the time. Fighting each other. Fighting to stay alive. Fighting for food. Learning to steal. Chrissie finding us a place to stay on skid row. Getting better at stealing. Getting really good at it. Then getting caught aged eighteen and getting eight months. Out barely five months, turn nineteen. Take an English lit correspondence course and that's it. What a life.

There's only a couple of good times in the whole thing. One was discovering books. The other was him. The night I lost myself to his commanding presence. Marco Alessi. Trust me to obsess over a man who killed the nephew of a

Don. The man I'm supposed to steal from. I'm drowning because of him.

I scream at the top of my voice but the universe doesn't respond. All I can do is die. I lay on my back and try not to panic. Water splashes over me but I keep breathing. What else can I do?

I don't know how long later but out of nowhere I see a light coming toward me. It gets nearer and I see it's a rowing boat. By now I'm starting to fade. It's a mirage. Last synapses shutting down. The cold has seeped deep into my bones and I'm way beyond shivering. I can't feel anything. Blinking seems to take minutes.

Turning my head toward the boat takes the last of the energy I have left. The light gets nearer and I try to call out but my throat's clogged with salt. Is it real?

I can feel my eyes closing and I get a horrible feeling this is it.

A wave rises and falls and then the boat's next to me. It hits my side and at least it's real. Too late but it's real.

"Hold on," a booming voice calls out. An arm reaches out and grabs me, holding me tight. "You're safe now." That's the last thing I hear for a very long time.

SIX

ELLIE

I wake up and the first thing I notice is I'm warm. I didn't think I could ever feel warm again. Close on the back of that feeling is the fact I'm alive. I'm not just alive, I'm out of the water.

Where the hell am I? I look around me. I'm on a bed, a four-poster bed like something out of a medieval castle. Am I dead and in heaven? Or hell? In heaven I wouldn't be tied up.

My hands are bound with zipties around my wrists. Same for my ankles.

I'm out of my clothes and wrapped up just in towels. My hair's dry so I've been here a while. Am I naked underneath the towels? I get the feeling I am. Someone stripped me and then tied me up. Who the hell would do something like that?

I need to pee and my throat's dry as desert sand. My limbs ache and they're itching like I'm about to get cramp. I'm guessing that's my nerves coming back to life. It used to be like that on the streets when we were freezing cold and then went in the library to warm up. Sometimes a church or shelter. Most often a fire in a dumpster that someone else had started. That was like this. Nerves itching but at least back then I could scratch. I can't do anything about this.

I crane my neck and try to work out where I am from the clues. Four-poster bed. Soft white blankets. Thick crimson carpet. Wood-panelled walls with paintings of landscapes wherever I look. One door. Shuttered windows. Nothing else. Not a single other thing in here.

I shove my body upward but I'm not just bound at the wrists and ankles. Ropes are attached to the zipties, thin cords that run to each corner of the bed. All I can move is my neck and not that much. What the fuck is going on?"

"Hello," I try to shout, shocked by how croaky my voice sounds. No one answers.

I don't know how long I'm laid here but by the time the door opens I'm dying to pee.

When it does open, my blood freezes in my veins. It's been a year, but I'd recognize that face anywhere. Bigger than last time I saw him, beard hiding his chin, hair a mess on top of his head. He's wearing a black suit and white shirt same as that day in the restaurant. "Marco?" I say as the enormous brute ducks to fit in through the door frame.

He saved my life. Rescued me from the water. My hero.

He's a coward, not a hero. Shot two children. Hiding out here, hiding from justice. A real piece of shit.

He nods. "I warned you what would happen if I saw you again," he says, closing the door behind you. "I told you I would keep you for good."

"Let me go," I say, tugging at the bonds holding me in place. I don't like the way he's looking at me. I like even less the way my body feels when I look at him. I don't want it to heat up like this. I don't want to feel desire when I'm tied down to a bed and unable to get away.

He walks toward me before stopping at the foot of the bed. "Why did you come here?" he asks.

"I don't even know where I am."

"You're in my house on my island. I'll ask once more. Why did you come here?"

"I didn't come here, genius. Someone brought me."

"That was me. I saw you falling overboard. Esposito sends someone after me and once again he sends you?"

I swallow hard. Fuck, he's handsome. Why does he have to look so handsome?

"Last chance," he says, running a finger along the rope that heads for my ankle. "Why are you here?"

"Let me go," I snap. "Let me go right now."

He shakes his head, like he's disappointed in me. "You seem to be under the misapprehension that you have a say in what happens to you while you're here. Let me clear that up right now. You are in my world and in my command. I could kill you right now and no one would care. You are no longer part of that world out there, Ellie. Your universe has contracted to this room and these four walls. Tell me the truth, Ellie." I frown and he grins. "Oh, yes, I know your name. I know all about you. I know you are studying. I know you live in a shitty apartment owed by my competitor. I know a lot about you but I do not know why you are here."

"Let me go."

"You will answer my questions when I ask them and if you don't, you will be punished. You remember what it was like to be punished by me, don't you, Ellie? Or have you forgotten already?"

I nod, my ass tingling at the memory. I can't admit how many times I've thought about that night, how often I've closed my eyes and used my vibrator and wished he would come back and finish what he started.

There is a beep from his jacket pocket. He pulls out his cellphone and glances at it. "I must deal with your associates. When I return, you better be willing to talk." He turns and walks out. The door locks a second later and I'm left still dying to pee, my body burning with a heat so fierce it's like I was never in the icy cold water at all.

SEVEN

MARCO

I can't believe she came to me. What was it Bogart said? Of all the houses on all the islands in all the world, she has to break in here? Or something like that.

Surely this is fate's way of giving me permission to keep her?

It was my cleaner who first saw their boat circling the island. He was up in the loft when he saw the lights out at sea. I have two staff. A cook and a cleaner. Ben and Horace. What are the odds Horace would be up there at the right time to see their lights? It's fate, I'm telling you. She's meant to be mine. My obsession came back and this time I'm not letting go.

Anglers sometimes come near this place but something about this boat didn't add up to Horace. Who goes fishing this late at night in weather like this?

I went to look from the shore and I saw her fall out when they hit the rocks. I was out in the rowing boat a minute later, forcing my way through the waves to get to her before she drowned. I dragged her onboard but she was already out cold. I rowed back and carried her to the house.

She looks as good as the last time I saw her.

When I first got her back to the island her temperature was dangerously low. I got her out of her wet things and wrapped up in the thickest towels I had.

At once her color started to come back, and she was muttering but the words made no sense. Something about debt and her sister and then something about Ferndean Manor. I give her a sedative and she's calm, settling to sleep.

The minute she came to she tried to run, scratched at me like she thought I was going to hurt her. I had to tie her down for her own safety. Then she passed out again. That's when I got the message from Horace. The boat she fell from reached the harbor.

This is my island. No one comes here without my approval. If they're here, it's because they want something. Me or her. They're getting neither.

I watch out for a while but I see nothing except the storm. I come back and get changed out of my wet things, go to see her a second time.

This time she's awake and looking at me with those eyes of hers that I could drown in. I'm going to punish her for coming back. I warned her not to.

I gave her a chance to run last time. She was just a kid back then. Barely eighteen. I'm fast approaching forty. She'd never be able to handle how intense I get, what I need from women.

It's a year later. She's back. She's going to find out why I warned her to stay away from me.

I'm going to fuck her. I'm going to make her choke on my cock, make those soft lips of hers taste everything I've got to give her. I'll watch her ass turn red under my hand, she'll moan my name, beg me to let her come.

She's climaxed once because of me and I know she's not forgotten. Thinks about it every single day. I only let her go last time because I had a war to deal with. Now all I want to do is be with her.

I know her name now. Found out easily enough. Eleanor Dalton. Apartment 12, Rose Street, Los Santos. She lied to me about her name but I can understand why. She was trying to lift my car keys. Working for my rival.

She'll end up dead. Don Esposito finds out about my obsession and she's dead. One woman of mine he's had killed in the past. Charlotte. I was only eighteen. That was before I became Don.

Got hit by that car. Esposito found the driver and handed him over. The driver talked, told me Esposito hired him to do it. I go to confront him and come back to find the driver's gone as if he never existed.

Esposito is laughing and calling me paranoid, asking why he'd do such a thing? Don told me to let it go. Don't provoke a war. Warned me that's what happens when you get close to women. Told me to keep my distance. Use them and lose them. Simple system. I never got close to another woman again. I couldn't risk it. I fuck and I move on.

As time went by Esposito got more powerful. All my time was taken up in keeping his family at bay. They were always trying to make inroads into our territory. He took up with selling powder and got even richer. We refused to deal in drugs. We have standards.

It ended in war. We managed to win, but the Don died. I took over, bided my time. So when Esposito's nephew gets killed on a bank job I approved, no wonder he blamed me. The bank was in my territory and I approved the job in return for a fifty percent cut of the take. First chance for Elda to prove himself. Show the truce is still intact.

Elda killed two children. I watched him do it. He came out of the bank with the cops running after him and tried to lose himself in my streets. Sneaked down past a kindergarten twenty feet from my place and the kids were looking out at him when he took his mask off.

He saw them looking. I yelled at him not to do it and he saw me yelling but he shot them both anyway, straight in the face. "Saw what I looked like," he says when he finally runs up to me.

I didn't hesitate. I got him inside, waited for the sirens to die down. Then I cut him up. Bastard deserved it for what he did. Found out later they were only four years old. Whole lives ahead of them. My territory and I'd promised their parents they were safe. I protect my people. Couldn't protect them though.

I moved out here the next day. I knew Esposito would come gunning for me. Turned my back on that world, left everything in Poletti's hands. He knows the family well enough, he's worked for us for decades. He can handle things. Had to go through Gianni turf at Gordon's Cove but Don Gianni is a decent enough guy. He's got his own fights. He doesn't need other people's.

When Esposito has calmed down, I'll go get him. He's too on edge at the minute, guards everywhere. I want him to think I'm scared, fearing for my life. Get him complacent. Make him think he's got me cowed. Then I take him out. Don't know how yet but I'll work it out. Only way to be safe. Cut the head off the hydra. Whack Don Esposito and our family is the only one in the game. The city is ours.

He's found out where I'm hiding though. Sent her to get me. As far as I can tell she's either an assassin or a honey trap. She's got a record. She knows how to lie. She's tried it before. A lesser man would have fallen for it, fallen for her pleading. Don't touch me. Don't spank me. I know the real her. She's a true submissive. She just doesn't know it yet.

At least I know she isn't wearing a wire. Nowhere to hide it on a naked body. Damned fine body too. I'll get her to talk when I get the chance. I'll use the methods I know so well to make her talk. Pleasure and pain. She won't be able to keep her mouth shut for long.

Before that I need to deal with the boat. It's already docked. I've alarms ringing the shoreline and they tell me the crew landed on the dock on the north side. It's the furthest point from the house so maybe they thought they could get here without being spotted. How dumb do they think I am? I haven't survived this long without taking precautions.

I check the cameras on infrared. Three of them, stepping onto my island like they belong here.

They won't leave this place alive.

They're tooled up. I can see them on the camera, checking their weapons, getting ready to move. They're coming to the house. No doubt they've been sent to kill me in revenge for Elda's death.

Someone found out about her somehow, worked out that she means something to me. Sent her to keep me occupied while those three sneak up behind me. Only they fucked up twice. Got seen by Horace. Then they scraped their boat on the rocks and sent her flying overboard.

I take one knife and the Glock. I shouldn't need anything else. There's only three of them.

I head out of the house and make my way along the track, past the old well, over to the north side of the island. I keep to the shadows and the storm makes life easy. They're never going to see me coming.

I sink into the darkness, watching, waiting. My breathing slows down. I've done this countless times before. It's surprising how quickly it all comes back. This is all I am. I'm a killer. Plain and simple. I remember what I learned over the years. No compassion. No mercy. Mercy is for the weak, to quote the Karate Kid. I always thought Cobra Kai should have won. I mean, no kicks to the head and Daniel wins with a fucking kick to the head? Cheating mother-fucker in my book.

The wind is howling and the rain lashes down. The hood over my head keeps my eyes clear of water. I grip the gun loosely, ready to move in an instant.

It should only take two minutes from the boat to here but ten go by and there's still no sign of them. I realize they must have taken a different route. I get up, moving quickly toward the shore. When I get there, I can see their boat but there's no sign of the three of them. I look back at the house. Muddy footsteps sweeping west, going wide. I march back.

Where are they? A shadow flickers across one of the windows. Not Horace or Ben. I'd recognize their outlines.

They're already inside.

Esposito will have sent his best, pure killers, same as me. She's not a killer though so what's she here for? Must be a distraction. Won't work. I'm focussed.

They'll be looking for me in there but I'm nowhere to be found. I'm out here looking in.

I hope they're ready because I'm coming for them.

EIGHT

ELLIE

I've done a lot of jobs in my time. This wasn't supposed to be any different. Get in, disable the alarms. Get the painting. Get out.

Instead, I'm tied to a bed with no way out and an insane Italian man lurking out there somewhere. He's Marco Alessi, mafia Don, child killer.

I look around the bedroom. My bladder is bursting and I'm furious. How dare he tie me to the bed? Who does he think he is?

When the door finally opens I'm ready to hurl abuse in his direction but it's not him, it's Sergio. "What the fuck happened to you?" he asks, walking over to me and licking his lips. "Say, you got anything on under those towels?"

"Untie me," I tell him. "Quick, before he comes back."

"Sure thing, dollface." He reaches into his pocket and pulls out a switchblade. He makes short work of the zipties around my wrists and ankles. The whole time he's staring at my body. I sit up, pulling the towels tighter around my chest. "Where are my clothes? You seen them?"

"What the fuck happened?" he replies. "One minute you're underwater and the next you're naked in here?"

"Clothes, now!"

"I was looking for Benito and Arlo, you see. They were supposed to be sweeping the second floor but there's no sign of them. Looks like the Marco's gone missing too."

I get off the bed, still holding the towel tight to me. I don't like the way Sergio's looking at me. "Let's go," I say, looking out into the corridor. "Any other bedrooms along here?"

The corridor has several doors either side of it. Sergio nods toward the nearest one. I push it open and it's identical to my one only there's a wardrobe near the window. I pull it open and get lucky. There are enough things in there for me to sling together an outfit. No underwear but I can get by for the short time I'm here. I pull out a light summer dress in yellow and white. It's halter neck with too much cleavage on show but what choice do I have? It's not exactly a fashion parade. There's a bathroom too so I duck into it and pee, sighing with relief. The pain was agony.

"Wait outside," I tell Sergio as the bathroom door creeps open.

"I should keep guard," he replies. "Make sure you don't go missing too."

"Get out!" I walk into the bedroom and point. He walks out like a beaten dog. I slam the door shut in his face. I drop the towel and slip into the dress in the time it takes him to get the door open again. I can see the look of disappointment in his face. "Let's get going," I add, not liking the way my tits are pressing against the fabric. I need something bigger to wear. This is clinging to me in all the wrong places. I push past him into the corridor. "Where's the study?"

"Downstairs and to the left."

"Anyone else here but Marco?"

"Horace and Ben."

"Where are they?"

"No idea. I've been listening out, but it's a fucking ghost house. You're the first person I've seen since getting in here."

"What if they've gotten hold of Benito and Arlo? You thought about that?"

"Will never happen. My guys are pros. You focus on the painting. I've got permission to shoot you if you try anything else. Maybe bear that in mind."

I think about my sister. What does she see in this guy? He's staring straight down my top the entire time he's talking.

I take the stairs down and step out into another long corridor. "Door at the end of the hall," Sergio whispers in my ear. "You hear that?"

I listen. There's the creak of a floorboard somewhere far above us. "I'll check it out," he tells me. "Be ready to go in two minutes."

He pulls out a gun and heads back upstairs. I walk along the corridor and stop outside the study. I know which room it is. Only one with a window above the door. I look back along the corridor. There's a plinth with a Roman-looking statue on it. I put the statue on the floor and then drag the plinth over. It's narrow but it'll do. I'm light enough on my feet.

I clamber onto it and balance at the edge, leaning toward the window above the door. I give the pane a shove and it opens enough for me to climb through. I'm glad Sergio's gone. I'm flashing everything up my dress. I'm glad to get through, get my legs back together.

I drop lightly down on the other side.

I did it. I'm in Marco Alessi's study.

The place smells like the library and my olfactory senses get wired up wrong with my desire. I'm back in the library again, dreaming of him. I shake my head. I'm here to do a job. Not to look at all those books.

There are bookcases lining all the walls except behind the worryingly tidy desk. Leather volumes. Old looking. I force myself to look at the painting.

It's old but I'm not sure how old. Looks pretty. A young girl no more than five or six, sitting on a wooden chair, facing the artist. She's got red hair similar to mine, and she's smiling. Looks like hundreds of other portraits I've seen. Not signed.

Above is a light shining onto it, low-watt bulb to protect the paint. That's where I'd run the cabling for the alarm. Actually, if it was a painting I thought was going to be stolen I'd have motion sensors. I can't see any. He's pretty lax, like he never saw this coming.

I walk over to the painting and I'm about to touch it when I hear a gunshot. It's faint. Somewhere far away. It's enough to make me pause. I don't like that sound. Who's shooting and why?

I can't hear any screaming. I run over to the door and put my ear to it. Nothing.

Do I leave the painting? try to get out of here? I watched Sergio piloting the boat. It didn't look too tricky. I could get back to the mainland and leave this place behind. But then what happens to Christine? Will I get shot if Sergio finds me running?

I don't stop to think any longer. I just work. I get to the painting and glance at the frame. Artex 3000 control panel over in the corner, hidden behind a potted plant. I run over and disable it. Takes seconds when you know what you're doing.

I lift the frame off the wall, put it down on the desk. Getting the painting out takes moments. Only clips holding it in place. There's something about that I can't put my finger on but I don't let it bother me. I'm listening out for more shots. I get the painting out and roll it up like a poster. Get a rubber band from his desk tidy. Wrap it up. With the painting under my arm I drag the heavy leather chair over to the door.

I lift my head just enough to peer out the window. I can't see anything but an empty corridor. Wherever the shooting was, it was far away. I don't give a shit anymore. All I need to do is get to the boat and get the fuck out of here before it's too late. Get back, hand over the painting, get my sister free and forget about all of this. By the morning I'll just be an honest student again. Put this behind me. Put Marco behind me. Try to forget him.

Is he in the house somewhere? Is he in one of these rooms right now? Fast asleep? Naked maybe?

I can't possibly stay. I'm stealing from him for one thing. For another my sister is in trouble. I can't stay. Part of me wants to though, no point denying it. Wants him to grab me and tell me I'm going nowhere.

There's something about his strength that does things to me, like he's a force of nature. It's as if I'm just a flower bending in the elemental gales coming my way. I can't stand up against it any more than I could stand up against him a year ago. He spanked me and it was an experience I never forgot no matter how much I tried to erase it from my mind.

The thing is I'm not the submissive type. I'm not a

woman who lets men tell me what to do. Too long fighting for myself against the world. I don't need anyone. Just me.

Then he comes along and I realize it's all a lie. I want to submit. I want him to take without asking. Just yank my panties off in the middle of the night, put a hand over my mouth, make it happen without a word. That way I don't have to feel guilty about submitting. I won't have to over-think anything.

All I'll have to do is let it happen, let him do whatever he wants to me. Give me another orgasm like that one in the restaurant that day. God, that was so good. Better than any I've ever had.

I knew he could rip me apart with his bare hands but instead those huge fingers were between my legs, a light blur on my clit when the boys I've known in the past have mauled me as if I was a games console controller.

I shake my head. I need to stop thinking about him. I've been frozen for too long. I need to move.

I drop the painting through the window and then climb out after it. I drop onto the plinth and then the floor. I pause, listening hard. Nothing. I realize I've no bearings to go by. Which way is the boat? How big even is this island? How big's the house?

I run along the corridor with the painting in my hand, looking for an exit. Around the corner, I stop. There's a body in the middle of the carpet. I walk toward it. That's Benito. He's got an expression on his face like he's surprised.

What happened to him? The carpet squelches under my feet. It's blood, and it's on my feet. I freak out, almost screaming. I get a hand to my face in time. Noise will give away my location.

It's not the first dead body I've seen in my life but this

one scares me. Who killed him? Was it Marco? There's no gunshot wound to go by. How did he even die?

I step over him. There's no time to think about those things. I need to get out of here. If Marco killed Benito for breaking in here, what's he going to do to me when he finds out I have his painting?

At the end of the corridor there's an entrance hall. It's filled with statues and paintings, the floor made of marble. Double doors lead outside. I pull the right-hand one. Locked.

My heart sinks but the left one swings inward when I try it. The wind hits me straight away and the rain sprays into the hall. The painting will get ruined if I go out there without protecting it.

Cursing silently, I run back to the corridor and try the nearest door. It's a billiard room. A baize table sits in the center of the space. Leather benches surround it. Nothing I can use to protect the painting. I pull open a cupboard but it only has pool cues inside. I run back out and try the next room. It's a closet and there's crockery on the top shelf, cutlery in drawers at the bottom. Useless.

The next door, I get lucky. It's a cloakroom filled with big heavy coats. I shove one over my shoulders and then grab another, wrapping it around the painting. Then I go back to the front door and run out.

I take a single step into the darkness when a hand grabs me. "Got you," a voice growls. I look to my left and Marco was there the whole time, waiting patiently for me to come out.

He's soaking wet from the rain, eyes glinting in the light shining out of the hall. His lips are set hard, and he's staring at me without blinking. He's got murder in his eyes.

Fear rises up in me as he tightens his grip on my wrist just like he did back in the restaurant. It's a grip I've no chance of escaping. "Come with me," he says coldly, yanking me back inside. "It's time for me and you to have a little talk."

NINE

MARCO

I need to talk to her. I also need to get rid of the bodies.

Disposing of the crew will be easy. There's the old well on the north side of the island. They walked right past it. Hasn't been used for a hundred years. Anything going into the bottom of that isn't coming out again. Dump them in there and get Ben to concrete it up.

I didn't get to become Don by being a wholesome human being. I got here by being ruthless. No compassion. No mercy. That's why the three men are dead. That's why I don't give a shit about what happens to their bodies.

So why am I letting her live?

She came with them. I should kill her too.

I left her locked in the bedroom, yelling to be let out. It's not happening yet. The window's locked and barred. All the windows in the place are barred except the skylights in the attic. She'd be doing well to get up there and even if she does, they're locked up tight.

She's not getting out. The bedroom door's solid enough to withstand her slamming against it as many times as she likes. She'll get tired, eventually. When she gives up the yelling, that's when we'll talk.

For now I need to get rid of the bodies. They'll stain the carpets and I can't have that.

I know all three of them. I haven't seen them for years but I don't forget faces easily.

Arlo was a merc. One of the best, back in the day. He was in the doorway when I got back to the house. He was supposed to be watching out, but he was typing something on his cellphone.

I got behind him and broke his neck before he even knew I was there. I left his body in the bushes and then checked his cellphone. Esposito was asking if the job was done yet. Proof Esposito set this up. Had they got the painting and was I dead? Arlo was in the middle of replying.

We're here. No sign of...

He never got to finish his thought. I silenced his cellphone and then broke it into pieces. Time to deal with the other two.

I knew there was only the three of them. The footprints in the wet mud running up to the house proved it.

I found Benito in the corridor on the first floor, not too far from the kitchen. He was the best of the crew. Used to do all Esposito's toughest jobs. Killed a senator in the middle of a parade and walked away. Famous for never getting a scratch on him.

He was walking the other way, looking for me, gun in hand. I tossed a knife which struck him between the shoulder blades. He went down groaning but not for long. He was on his knees when I pulled the knife out. He rolled onto his back and the last thing he saw in this world was me looking down at him, watching him die. "But I'm the best," he said, looking confused.

"Not anymore," I replied, kicking the gun out of his hand. He lunged up for me, using the last of his strength. I got the knife into his throat and yanked it down and out. He was dead a second later.

I was heading upstairs to look for Sergio when I heard him talking to Ellie. She was giving him a mouthful, and I wanted to go and snap his neck but not yet. I needed to get him alone. She didn't need to see him die.

I climbed the servants' staircase and deliberately hit the creaking floorboards on the way, bringing him hunting for me. He had his gun out when he appeared but he didn't see me. I was watching him from behind the fire hose. By the time he spotted me I'd already fired. He got off a couple of wild shots but both mine hit home. Down he went, his eyes already blank by the time I kicked his gun out of his hand.

That just left her. I knew she'd want to get to the boat and get gone as fast as possible so all I had to do was wait by the front door. She showed up and I got hold of her, dragged her back inside, carried her up to the bedroom. Might keep her there for a while. Maybe for good.

She's been a bad girl, trying to steal from me. Tried to take *Girl in Chair*. The one thing Esposito wants more than anything else in the world. The one thing he can't have. My painting. I'm keeping it. Keeping her too.

I leave her to her yelling and ignore the stiffening of my cock at the thought of her in there, deserving punishment. Work first, then pleasure.

I get Arlo's body out to the van. Ben's waiting there, wrapped up in a waterproof coat with the hood up, smoking silently, shielding the cigarette with his hand. He nods my way. "Want some help?"

"I made the mess. I'll clean them."

"How come you don't say that about the dishes?" he calls after me as I head back to gather up Benito. The body is heavy but nothing I can't handle. I can still hear her yelling in her bedroom. She's clearly not worn herself out yet.

I get Benito into the back of the van and then I go get Sergio. I'll have the boat scuttled in the morning and that'll be that. Just me and her to have some fun.

She won't ever be able to leave without my permission. I've got my own boat and the chopper but she's not getting in either without my say so. I'm not giving it anytime soon. She's been too bad. She's going to be punished for a long time.

I load Sergio into the van and then Ben drives us out to the well. The tires slip through the mud. I sit in the passenger seat and look out at the darkness. "You back at work already?" Ben asks when he finishes his cigarette. "We only just got here."

"Nope," I reply. "They came for *Girl in Chair*."

"Told you, unless Esposito's dead, he'll keep trying to get it."

I say nothing. He'll get it when the time is right and not before.

The van stops and we open the back. Ben gets the cover off the well and I carry the bodies over one by one. Shoving them down, I see nothing in the dark but I hear the splash when they hit the bottom, one after another.

When we're done, we get the cover back on and then drive to the house. Ben turns to me once we're in the entrance hall. "You want me to deal with the carpets?"

"Get Horace to help. He knows what to use on them. Concrete the well when it stops raining. Plenty of cement in the garage."

"Got it."

He heads for the staff quarters. I walk upstairs. Ellie is quiet at last. Looks like she's finally given up yelling. I unlock the door and push it open. I don't see her at first. My mistake. I didn't check my corners. Maybe I'm getting sloppy.

She pounces from behind the door and tries to get her fingers into my eyes. She's climbing up my spine, hurling abuse. I press back against the wall, crushing her in place. "You going to be nice?" I ask, peeling her hands off my face.

"Fuck you," she replies but already the breath is leaving her. I hear her breathing change as she notices I'm covered in blood. "What happened to you?" she asks. "Is that your blood?"

I lower her to the ground, kicking the door shut, blocking it with my body so she can't run. "Your crew are all dead," I tell her. "And unless you want to follow them, tell me the truth about why you came to my island."

"I'm not telling you anything."

"That's my painting downstairs, isn't it? You come to steal *Girl in Chair* for Esposito? He tell you why he wants it so bad? Let me guess. He told you I stole it and he just wants it back, right?" I take a step toward her. There's nowhere for her to go.

She's pressing herself back against the wall, staring at me with a mixture of anger and fear in her eyes. Her hands are outstretched, trying to fend me off but she's no strength compared to me. "I just killed three men," I say. "What makes you think I won't kill you?"

Her face crumbles. "Please...please don't kill me."

I turn away to lock the door, pocketing the key once that's done. There's a sink in the room's corner. I cross to it and wash my hands, watching the blood run down the plughole.

"How many people have you killed?" she asks, her voice quiet. "Altogether?"

"After a while, you lose count. The bodies blend into one." I dry my hands and then face her.

She's trying the door. "It's locked," I tell her, holding the key out with my hand. "If you want out, you're going to tell me everything I want to know."

"I'm not telling you anything."

"Why protect him?"

"Who? Sergio?"

"Esposito. He's not a man you can trust. What did he offer you? Money? How much?"

"I don't know what you're talking about."

"I'm done with your lies." I march over and grab her. She tries to fight me but I don't let go. I drag her over to the bed and bend her over it. "Remember being in this position before?"

I yank the back of her dress up to reveal she's got no panties on. Not surprising. She stole the dress. Stole from the leftover clothes of the few women who've been allowed to come here.

None of them ever got to stay more than a night. Not her though. She's staying a lot more than one night. I might never let her leave. I slap my hand down on her ass, my other arm keeping her in place.

"Let me go!" she shouts.

"You said that last time," I reply. "Came for me a few minutes later for me though, didn't you?"

"Fuck you."

"Such a mouth on you but we'll fix that. Fix many things tonight. First of all your delusion that you have a say in things." I spank her again, loving the sound of my hand slapping her ass. My cock is already throbbing with desire at the sight of her perfect peachy behind. I kick her ankles apart and there's that pussy I never forgot. Looks like it's glistening already. I was right. She likes the pain.

"Say sorry for lying to me," I tell her, spanking her again. "Say it."

"Let me go."

"I can improve your life if you work with me," I say, letting my hand slide between her legs, finding her clit and then brushing lightly over it. "Say sorry."

"Never," she snarls but her voice is weaker. Her breathing has changed and it changes again when I spank her this time. She pushes her ass back instead of trying to shift away. I stroke her clit and she twists her neck to look at me. "Please let me go," she says, the tone of her voice completely different.

For a moment I almost do it. That's the hold she has over me. One request with those big doe eyes and I nearly crumble. Fucking lucky she's not a honey trap. I'd have blabbed all my secrets already.

"Say sorry." I slap her ass over and over again, my hand stinging from the repeated blows. She starts to yell and curse but I don't stop. "I can keep going all night," I tell her. "Must be starting to hurt by now."

Her buttocks are bright red and she's taking more than I expected but she crumbles in the end. I knew she would. "All right," she says, half crying, half defiant. "I'm sorry, all right."

"And what are you sorry for?"

"I don't know. Whatever you want. Just stop spanking me."

"Why? You seem to like it." I stroke her clit again. Her

pussy is soaking wet and my cock twitches, wanting to be inside her.

"Please, don't."

I let go of her. She turns around, her eyes glistening with frustration and fear.

"It's funny," I say as she tugs her dress back down into place. "You say you want me to stop but you look pissed at me when I do. You want to know what I think?"

"No."

"I think you like the pain. I think you know you've done a bad thing and you know you have to be punished for it. I think you want to submit to me and you know what else?"

"What?"

"You're not leaving my island until you do."

TEN

ELLIE

I want to hate him. I do hate him. But I want him more. Every spank that lands on my ass sends shockwaves through my body and my mind.

I can't get away from him. That's the worst part. Even if I could work my way loose from his overwhelming grip, I can't get off his island. Who owns an island anyway? What is he, a Bond villain?

Focus.

I can get to the boat. I can pilot it back to the mainland. Pilot it? Sail it? Doesn't matter. I might not know which direction to go but I reckon I can work it out. Anything's better than staying here with a murderer who chills my blood as much as he heats up my body.

I have to get away from him. If I stay here any longer, there's a real risk I might not want to leave.

What he's doing is intoxicating. It seeps into my bones, changes who I am. Makes me want to submit to him.

It doesn't help that he's so arrogant, a mature, confident

man who knows exactly what he wants out of life. He wants me. Obsessed with me, it seems.

I'm draped over the bed with my ass in the air and the dress around my waist and he's stopped spanking me at last.

I'm fighting for my breath, hardly able to believe I just apologized to him.

Can I tell him the truth? What will he do if I admit I am here to steal his painting?

He knows that already. It's not like I could tell him I was just taking the painting out of the frame to air it. He must know I'm a thief.

What I need to do is get away from here before it's too late. I can't stay. Staying means admitting that he's right, means accepting that I do like the pain, that I deserve the punishment he's meting out.

Damn him. I wish I'd never met him. My life was so much simpler before he walked into it. Miserable at times, sure. But at least it was simple.

He's pushing his hand between my legs, stroking my clit and I'm melting under his touch. I want this to stop. I need it to. If it doesn't, I'm going to come again and I can't. I can't let him turn me into the sex obsessed sub he thinks I am.

I try to shove my legs closed but he's got his knee there, keeping them apart. "You're going to come for me," he says, slipping his finger around my clit in ways that make me moan out loud. "You're going to come with my fingers inside you because you're a dirty little girl, aren't you? What are you?"

"Fuck you," I manage to say but my words are weakening as much as my resolve. I hate my own body for betraying me like this. He's doing things to me he has no right to do but my body's reacting anyway.

"You trying to say you don't like this?" He slips a finger

into me and brings it out again, showing me the wetness that coats it. "What's that if not your enjoyment?"

I stand upright but it's the worst thing I could have done. He grabs hold of me and pulls me toward him, pressing his body against mine. "You feel that?" he asks.

I know exactly what he's talking about. His cock is pressing against me, hard and huge. I can't think about anything else. I want it inside me. I know I shouldn't.

Everything about this whole situation is wrong. He's just killed three people. I should be running for my life but instead I want him in me and I hate myself for having such a thought.

He leans down, and his lips are an inch from mine. "I know you want me," he says. "Just tell me the truth. Why do you want my painting so bad? What did Esposito offer you in return for it? You've been going straight for a while. Started college. He must have offered you something good to get you on this job. What was it? Money? I can give you more."

"You can't give me what I want."

"Try me."

I try to pull away from him but he's got one arm around my waist, holding me in place. "Let me go," I snap, shoving at his arm.

"Not until you tell me the truth."

"What does it matter? You caught me, all right. So just call the police and get this over with. Stop torturing me."

"I'm not torturing you. I'm disciplining you."

"What's the difference?"

"A torturer cares only about inflicting pain. I care about teaching you right from wrong. Your punishment matches your crime and you will learn from it."

"Learn what exactly? That you're a murdering piece of shit?"

"Learn to do as you're told when you're in my company." He strokes a hand through my hair. I've always had a thing about that. His thick fingers brush my scalp and shudders run down my spine. Even his forearms look good. I feel safe in them. I hate that feeling.

He's so huge, I feel tiny compared to him, like he could snap my neck or toss me out of the nearest window without any effort at all. The fear laces everything I feel.

I'm in his power and I am scared but there's something else running through my head as well. It's a voice that tells me to give in to him, let him do this. With no need to play any part in things, I can just do as I'm told, like he says. Do as I'm told and enjoy myself.

Submit to him. Agree to this.

I need to get away. I don't like that voice. I don't want it to have any control over me. I don't want him to have control over me. I am my own person. I can look after myself.

"You need this," he says, taking hold of the back of my neck, leaning down and pressing his lips roughly to mine.

He kisses me deeply, his tongue plunging straight into my mouth. I go rigid in his grip but then, so help me, I kiss him back. I melt into his arms as his hand slides down my back to cup my bare ass under the dress.

He's staring into my eyes the entire time. I can't stand that stare. It's too intense.

I shut my eyes, forgetting everything but the kiss. It's so filled with passion, so different to every embrace I've had before. They were boys, tentative, groping, nervous. This is a man. A man who knows what he's doing.

I shudder again, this time at the thought of being fucked

by this man. He's not a man who makes love. He's a man who fucks.

His hands are pulling at the dress, lifting it up over my tits. I try to push it back down into place but he shoves my hands away. "I take it off you or I rip it off you," he growls.

I know he means it. The dress comes over my head and gets tossed aside. I'm naked in front of him and his eyes burn into my body. He presses himself against me again, his tongue once more claiming my mouth. It's all the more obscene because he's still fully dressed in that suit of his.

If there's one thing I've learned over the years it's how to think fast. Even as he's kissing me I'm thinking. I need to get off this island. The best way to do that is with the boat.

How do I get to the boat?

I have to get out of the house first.

How?

Wait until his guard is down.

I will wait until the time is right and then run.

"I know what you're thinking," he says. "I will give you the painting when you leave."

"I want to leave now."

"Do you?" He runs a hand down between my legs. "Your body suggests otherwise."

Out of nowhere he grabs me and tosses me onto the bed. Before I've even landed he's pouncing on me, shoving my legs apart. "You're going to tell me the truth," he says, his hot breath on my pussy a moment later. "I'll make sure of it."

He spreads my lips apart. "Perfect," he says, running his tongue up and over my clit.

I gasp, pushing my hips up to meet his face. All thoughts of leaving drop out of my head. All I care about is his touch on me. I don't know what it is about it but there's something about the way he handles me that is like nothing I've ever known.

It's happening just like it did at the restaurant. I'm losing control of myself. "Come for me," he says. "Come for me, Ellie."

His tongue starts circling my clit. He pushes a thick finger into me at the same time. It takes mere moments to reach my climax. My back arches as I push my body against him, waves of pleasure washing over me. "I'm coming," I manage to say but then I can say nothing else. I can only gasp with pleasure.

He stands up in front of me, unzipping his pants. "Are you on the pill?"

I nod, swallowing hard, my face burning up as my climax continues to wash over me.

"For now." The sight of his cock as he pulls it out almost tips me over the edge a second time. It's rigid and thicker than I expected, pointing aggressively toward me. He strokes it hard, like how he gripped my wrist. "You want this in you, don't you?"

I want to shake my head but I can't do it. "Please," I manage to say. "Let me go."

"No chance." He climbs onto the bed, the sheer size of him threatening to crush me. He supports himself on one arm, the other moving between us. He guides his cock toward my pussy, staring into my face the entire time. "What do you want my painting for?" he asks.

"I need it to save my sister," I reply, the words slipping out before I can stop them.

His expression changes. He frowns slightly as he looks down at me. "Explain."

It feels odd to do it with the tip of his cock on my clit but the words fall out in a rush. "She owes some guy money, and he said he'd write off the debt if I collected Girl in Chair for him."

"Don Esposito. Why you though? Why send you?"

"Because he knows I used to be a cat burglar."

He leans down and plants a soft kiss on my lips. It's the last soft thing that happens to me. "You can earn that painting," he says," by submitting to me."

I go to answer but the breath is knocked from me as he slides his cock straight into my waiting pussy. He thrusts his hips until he's all the way inside me. Once he's sure I've adapted to the size of him, he speeds up, slamming back and forth, his pelvis grinding against my clit.

I find myself clawing at his back, wrapping my legs around him, pulling him in deeper. He fills me in a way nothing ever has, stretching inside me painfully until I expand to accommodate him.

The entire time he's slamming into me, he's still staring at me. "Going to come in you," he says as he slows his hips, teasing me by rocking back and forth halfway into me. "You ready for it?"

"Give it to me," I say in a voice I don't recognize. It's more forceful, much bolder than I've ever been in bed.

"Call me Sir."

"Give it to me, Sir."

"Tell me to come inside you."

"Come in me, Sir."

He thrusts faster and faster, grinding against me and I feel my own body heating up in response. I know what's going to happen and I want it so badly, I ache in the pit of my stomach. I know I should run from this man and not look back but in this moment all I can do is let him do this.

He's pinned me to the bed anyway. I'm not going

anywhere until he's finished with me. Not that I want to go anywhere. Not anymore.

His breathing turns into grunts, and then he leans down and plunges his tongue into my mouth. In the same instant he thrusts all the way inside me and it happens. He comes deep into me, his cock spurting hot wetness as my own body responds, climaxing a second later, squeezing the last drops from him.

He slides out at once, standing up again, pushing his still twitching cock back into his pants. "Get some sleep," he says. "We'll talk more in the morning."

A second later he's left the room, locking the door behind him. I'm left looking at the door and hating him more than ever. He just used me and then walked away. What kind of cold-hearted bastard does that?

That makes my mind up. I need to get gone and not look back. The only question is, how? The door's locked. The window's barred. I go pee and and then return to bed. I lay back and close my eyes. I'll work it out, somehow. I just need to think. That's what I do. I think my way out of problems. I can think my way out of this.

I close my eyes to concentrate, my dazed head filled with endorphins. Before I know it, I'm fast asleep.

ELEVEN

MARCO

I wake up early. That's not like me. My routine has remained the same on or off my island. Up at six and into the gym down in the basement. Breakfast is laid out for me for seven thirty and I'm showered in time to eat it.

This morning I'm awake at five.

I know why. It's because of her.

I thought of her the entire time I was settling last night. I'm already beyond obsessed. The first thought I have when I wake up is to go to her. I resist the temptation. She needs to learn patience and how am I supposed to teach her that if I can't stay away from her?

Patience is a virtue in my line of work. You wait for the right opportunity to get revenge. Look at Esposito. He thinks he's safe. He thinks I'm out of the game completely. I haven't told anyone my plan. Wait until his guard is down and then go pay him a little visit.

I need to get more information from her. If she's supposed to take him my painting to get her sister back, she must have a meeting point set up. A time to get there. The more information I have, the better I can plan the hit.

Her coming here means my plans can move forward. When she takes the painting to him will be the best time. His guard will be down. He'll think he's won. Maybe I should show myself in the city, make it look like I'm flitting in and out.

I'll get her onside, make her so submissive she won't even think about disobeying me. Then I'll send her in there as bait, wait until he's distracted before I make my move.

I smile to myself as I get out of bed. It's going to be a good day. I'm going to have breakfast with her and then show her what life with me is going to be like. I head down to the gym and get straight on the treadmill. Twenty minutes of fast running gets my heart pumping properly.

The entire time I'm thinking of her. Such a perfect body. The way she looks scared when I get close to her, like she's afraid I might kill her. As if I'd kill something so perfect. I'm keeping her, not killing her. Never going to let her go.

She's mine for life now. I decided last night I'm keeping her for good. She will become my wife after she's learned how to behave around me. I will do my utmost to break her in gently, show her the pleasure she can gain from submitting to my every command.

I will possess her. She already possesses my heart. Took it that night in the restaurant and never gave it back.

I don't need to check on her until breakfast is ready. I know exactly where she is.

I move onto the weights bench. Let her eat. Tell her what's expected of her. Lay out the rules for her stay. I just won't tell her the stay is permanent. Let her think she has a chance to get out of here.

She's locked in the most secure guest bedroom. There's no way she's leaving there until I allow it. She'll have to earn her freedom. If she's anything like she was last night, it won't be difficult.

She's so responsive to me, her body responding the right way even if her mouth responds with curses.

Seeing her reach orgasm did something to me I never expected. Made me feel something I've not felt for anyone else. I wouldn't call it love. I'm not the kind of man who falls in love. It is something strong though, a bond that formed between the two of us, a glue that seals us together.

The bond will become stronger soon. Once she's off her birth control.

She will give me children. The one thing I never thought I wanted. I never did, before now. She's changed me already. Made me think about things in a different way.

I get through my reps and then I shower and get dressed. It's not hard to choose when I own a lot of black suits and not much else except my gym gear. Once I'm done I check with Ben that he's prepping for two.

I head upstairs after that, walking the short distance to her bedroom, key in hand. There's no sound coming from inside. Is she still asleep?

I unlock the door and push it open. The covers look slept in but she's not there. Is she in the bathroom? She has to be. There's nowhere else she could be. The shower's running. I think about joining her in there. Not yet. Rules laid out first.

The bathroom door's locked so I knock once. "Come out now," I tell her, "Or I'm coming in."

There's no reply. I knock again. "Last warning."

Still no response.

I give the door a kick and it breaks off its hinges. I step

over it and look around me. She's not there. Where the hell is she?

I sweep the bathroom, making sure I've checked everywhere. The window is open but only the two inches it can go before it hits the bars on the other side. I turn around and walk back into the bedroom. I rip the covers off the bed and then toss the mattress to the side. She's neither in the bed nor under it. I look around me. The window is still secure.

How the hell did she escape from a locked bedroom?

TWELVE

MARCO

I stand in the corridor and think. How many doors in this place? She could be behind any one of them. If she can get out of a locked room, she can unlock any of those doors. She must be hiding somewhere. It's simply a matter of tracking her down.

I clench my fists. She's in big trouble when I get hold of her. She won't sit down for a week. I'm thinking this isn't a spanking offense. This is the paddle. Show her what happens when she makes me mad.

I look in the nearest rooms. No sign of her.

I think for a moment. She's not the type to hide where I'd expect. She's probably back in the bedroom. There's somewhere I haven't thought of, there must be.

I search again but there are no hiding places, no panels moved in the walls, nothing touched on the ceiling. The carpet is still in place. How the hell did she do it?

There's a beep on my cellphone. I pull it out and look at the alarms. The dock. Something's triggered the camera on the dock. I load the live camera in time to see the boat setting off. I zoom in and there she is, piloting the thing out of the harbor and into open water.

Fuck! I forgot to have it scuttled. I was too distracted by her.

Through my rage I manage a smile. She's done something I never would have predicted. Something no one's done before. She's managed to escape my island.

She won't be gone for long. I can see she's got the painting rolled up by her side as she works her way out into open water. I know something about it she doesn't, something that'll bring her back to me soon enough.

I could go after her but I'm not going to, not yet anyway. I punch her home number into the phone and call it. I leave her a message before hanging up. Once she gets to her apartment she'll listen to the message and realize she has no choice but to come back. Willingly or not.

I watch the camera until she's out of sight. I can't help but admire her. She managed to get out of a locked room. Not only that but while I was still trying to work out where she was hiding she was running for the dock. The front door is supposed to be uncrackable. I'm betting when I get down there it'll be wide open. She's an expert cat burglar. I'll give her that. Much better than her clumsy efforts in the restaurant would suggest.

The clock is already ticking. She just doesn't know it yet. She thinks her best shot at getting her sister free is to take Esposito's deal?

Her best shot is to get her ass back here and apologize, beg me to help her sort this mess out for her. I will too. For a price. The price is her. She will be mine. Esposito will be dead. Her sister will be free. Everyone will be happy.

I have a suite of rooms that I use whenever I have a

special guest. It's been a while so I go check everything is ready for her arrival.

The bedroom is ready, ropes laid out for me to tie her down. Punishment room is ready too. The red room. I look in the drawers. Butt plugs, paddles, and leather belts. Lube and vibrators. Gags, blindfolds, handcuffs.

I'll bring her back here to finish what we started.

She doesn't ring me. I give her until the evening but it doesn't happen. So I guess I'm going to have to go get her.

I sail to the mainland, find the Bentley missing. Never mind. It would have been too conspicuous anyway. I collect a Ford from the long stay parking garage, and set off. I punch her address into the GPS and make my way to the city. She's living in a slum block but not for much longer.

Soon she'll be on my island, in my house. She'll never leave without permission again. I'll teach her a lesson. Show her what happens when you disobey me.

It'll be a lesson she'll never forget.

THIRTEEN
ELLIE

He's not as smart as he thinks he is. His house isn't as secure either. I could see the methods he'd employed, and they were good but I'm better. I've needed to get into lots of different houses in my time. Once I got out of prison, I never expected to need to use these skills again but they've worked well for me today. Got me out instead of in but at least I'm free. That's what matters.

As I make my way back to the mainland, I keep looking back. I'm expecting him to chase after me. There's no sign of him. Maybe I'll get away with this. I have the painting. I have no reason to go back there. I'm free. Soon Christine will be free too and then I'm going to suggest the two of us move somewhere far away, start again.

Do I tell her about Sergio? That's not an easy question to answer. He was a piece of shit and now he's dead but she was engaged to him. She did love him. God knows why but she did. If I do tell her, I'll have to work out the right way to do it.

First things first, I need to get back to the mainland. I've no idea where I am but I can see the shore in front of me and what looks like a dock. Once I get there I need to call Esposito. My phone went over the side with me when I fell off the boat. I need to get a new one or get home and use the phone there. At least my handbag was still in the boat where I left it. Nothing identifiable in it, just my apartment key and a few quarters in my purse.

I look behind me again. Still no sign of him. That's what I don't like about this. He's unpredictable. I was sure he'd come after me when I escaped.

It was hard enough to keep quiet when he came into the bedroom. There I was hiding under the bed and the minute he unlocks the door I want to come out and apologize for hiding, beg for his forgiveness, get on all fours and present my ass for a spanking I deserve.

There's something seriously wrong with me. I blame the island. It's a contained environment. It's sent my internal wiring all over the place. I would never want to submit to someone like him normally. I don't want to. I want to get away from him and never see him again.

I feel a sharp pang of agony at the thought that I'll never see him again. Why do I even care? He's a man who doesn't listen when I say I don't want something. He's a brute, plain and simple.

He looked like a brute when he appeared in the bedroom. I used a hairpin to latch the bathroom door, make it look like I was in there with the door locked. He knocked and then kicked it down. The sheer strength of his kick terrified me. I wouldn't want to be on the receiving end of something like that.

As soon as he was out of sight in the bathroom, I was up and out from under the bed, running as quickly and quietly as I could. His front door was secured, but I wasn't a cat burglar for nothing. I got it open and was out and running for the boat at top speed seconds later. I followed the muddy footprints all the way to it. Sergio's prints leading the way. He'd never make any again.

The shoreline comes into view and I run through things in my head. Get home. Get changed. Call Esposito. Arrange the meeting. Hand over the painting. Get Christine out of there. Get gone.

Esposito had said it would only take one night, that I'd be home by the morning. He wasn't wrong, just not the way he probably expected. His three guys are dead and I'm the only survivor.

That's me. I'm a survivor.

I bring the boat into the dock and tie it up. This time of the morning there's only a couple of guys fishing off the end of the pier. Guy with a dog by his side waves at me. I wave back. Nothing to see here.

Gordon's Cove is a small town on the edge of the county. Nothing much happens here ever by the looks of things. I leave the boat and head over to the parking lot at the edge of the harbor.

There are some warehouses to my left, and cars parked up on my right. Up on the cliff top is a casino. I bet there's some nice cars up there. Down here in the long stay garage my pickings are slim. I walk between the rows until I find a Bentley that's unlocked. Nice. Maybe it's Marco's. That would be justice for what he's done to me. Hot wiring doesn't take long and then I'm driving out of town, heading back to the city.

The entire time I can't help thinking he's coming for me. Whenever I look behind me I expect to see him following but there's no one there. The road is empty. I feel strangely disappointed that he gave up so easily. Last night he seemed like he was obsessed with me yet today he just lets me go?

Not going to lie, I will miss the feeling of being the object of his obsession. It felt kind of good to know I can have that effect on someone. Even as he was punishing me, his whole attention was on me.

It's a feeling that's hard to get away from. I know he's bad news. Killed two kids. Ex-mafia. Or maybe not so ex. Cold, cruel, rough. Doesn't listen to the word no. I should run a mile. The red flags are waving so hard in my face that I can't see anything else.

Yet there's more to him than that. I can see behind those things to something deeper. There's a pain inside him, a pain I know. It's the thing that bonded us. He knows brutality and hardship and so do I. He's had to work hard to get where he is, that's obvious. Made some tough choices. Me too. Done things he's not proud of? Me too.

Still, it's better that he isn't following me. I'm not sure I could cope with that intensity for any real length of time. Better to just leave it all as a memory where it belongs.

I get a quarter of a mile from my place and dump the Bentley by the station in the no parking bays. It'll get picked up by the local cops and returned to Gordon's Cove soon enough. I'm not even going to try to sell it. I'm going straight. No more crime. All the owner will be down is the gas it took to get here.

I carry the painting inside my building and up the stairs to my place. I get my key out of my handbag and turn it slowly in the lock, listening hard. There's a chance he's inside.

No one's there. I get in and move through the entire place quickly, keys between my knuckles ready to lash out. It doesn't take long to search, the place isn't that big.

Bedroom, no one in there. I check under the bed. Just dust bunnies.

The bathroom is empty too, the faucet still dripping as if I never left.

That only leaves the lounge and kitchen, an all in one space with nowhere to hide but behind the sofa or the curtains. No one there. I'm alone. I'm safe.

I lock the door and lean back against it. The answer machine on the kitchen counter is blinking. I hit the button and listen.

"You have two new messages. Message one." Don Esposito's voice. "If you're back to hear this message, the job must be done. Well done, you. Six this evening. The Piazza. By the clock tower."

"Message two." Then the voice that makes my insides melt. It's Marco. "By now you've no doubt worked out the painting's a forgery. You want the real thing? You have until six this evening to come back here or I'm coming to fetch you." The line goes dead.

I unroll the painting. A forgery? It looks real enough but I'm no art dealer. Could he be bluffing? Is this his way of getting me to come back willingly? He knows my number. No doubt he knows my address. Shit, I'm in deep trouble here.

What am I supposed to do?

Think. That's what I do best.

Think fast.

I cross to the sofa and collapse onto it, the painting on my lap. I look down at it and weigh things up. Four options.

One, the painting is a forgery. I take it to Esposito and hope he doesn't notice.

Two, the painting is not a forgery. Marco is bluffing. I

take it to Esposito and hope he keeps his word and lets Christine go.

Three, the painting is a forgery and I go back to get the real one. Sneak onto the island and make sure I don't get caught this time.

Four the painting is not a forgery and I willingly climb back into the lion's den.

I examine the painting closely. There's nothing there to tell me whether it's real. I decide Marco's bluffing. He has to be. This is his way of getting me to come back but I'm not going to. I can't handle things on the island. They move too fast. He's too much.

The clock ticks on by and I'm still unsure what to do until it gets close to six. Screw it, I say to myself. I have to take the risk. I head out the door with the painting rolled up and make my way on foot to the piazza.

It's twenty minutes from my door and when I get there I see just one man by the clock tower. It's got to be him. I walk over and he's a guy in his mid-fifties, graying hair, sallow skin. He's got a droopy nose and droopier jowls. Light gray suit that looks expensive. It hangs loosely off him like he rarely takes it off, the creases well worn in.

He doesn't smile at me, simply glances at the painting and nods. "You must be Ellie," he says. "You look a lot like your sister."

"Where's Christine?"

"Hand over the painting first."

"Where is she?"

"She's safe, don't worry. Hand it over."

"I'm giving you nothing until I know she's all right."

He reaches into his jacket pocket. I wince, expecting to see a gun but instead he pulls out a cellphone. On the screen is footage of the interior of a van and sitting inside it is Christine, flanked by two dour looking men. She looks skinnier than last time I saw her. "Happy now?" he says, putting the cellphone away. "You hand the painting over, I wave, and that van parked over there opens up. Out she comes and off you two go, two happy siblings."

I look at where the van's parked. So close and yet so far. I pass him the painting. A smile lights up his face as he unfurls it. He pulls out a flick knife and scrapes at the paint at the foot of the chair. His smile turns into a bitter grimace. "What the fuck is this?" He's spitting with rage as he grabs my collar. "You try to cheat Lorenzo Esposito?"

I try to peel his hand from me but he's already let go. He waves at the van and it revs loudly, racing off into the distance. "What are you doing?" I ask. "We had a deal."

"You got me a fake." He hurls it to the ground. "Do you think I'm a fool? Did you and Marco cook this up together? Take advantage of an old man?"

"I got it off the wall in the study like you said. That was the painting that was there."

"You got me a fake." He wipes his mouth with the back of his hand, getting hold of his emotions. He takes a deep breath before continuing. "I'm not an ogre, Eleanor. I can be quite generous."

He writes a number down on a tiny notepad and then hands me the folded sheet. "You can have forty-eight hours to bring me the genuine painting. Call me when you have it. Fail and I bury your sister underground." He walks away, looking back over his shoulder to add with a chilling smile, "While she's still breathing."

FOURTEEN

MARCO

It's good to see the city again. The island is good for a man to rest, but it is not a place to live permanently. I belong here in the city. I grew up here. I know the streets. I know the people. I know the businesses. I know that Esposito wants to get his filthy hands on it all but he won't. I own it.

He owns some of the shittier parts. Like her building. The concrete at ground level is crumbling on the corners, those corners barely visible beneath the spray tags and ripped posters for bands that broke up ten years ago. Not a hint of green anywhere. Just concrete and chainlink fencing.

I've parked the Ford outside and I'm leaning back against it, looking up at the windows above me. Half of them cracked, no lights and no curtains in most of them. One or two shining. Which is hers?

Is she up there right now?

For the right money you can find out anything. I found

out her name, her numbers, her address. Everything I needed for this moment.

She's coming back with me. I want to stay in the city but the heat's too much right now. Esposito wants me dead and all his soldiers are on the lookout. Any one of his associates could get made if they're willing to whack me in the street. The Feds are sniffing around too. They want information about the bank job.

The guy who did it might be dead but they don't know that. All they know is two children are dead, and it took place on Alessi turf, right by my front door. That makes me a person of interest.

I've enough detectives in my pocket to keep the police off my back but the Feds are a different story. Too many of them pretend to be honest, pretend they give a shit about what's right and what's wrong. They poke their noses in long enough and they're sure to find something to pin on me.

So I'm not staying long. Just long enough to grab her and get her back to the island. Once she's locked in, properly this time, then I can make some plans.

I'm not letting her live here for another minute. She's moving to mine and staying. This shitty building can live without her.

I gave her until six and she never called, never reappeared. So matters are in my hands now. I just hope she hasn't gone to see Esposito with the forgery. She might never make it back.

I'm risking showing my hand a little more than I like. He sees it's a forgery and he'll know I'm on my guard. He wants to steal it but it's not his. It's mine. Like her. She's mine. Anyone gets in my way and they'll be spraying blood all over the sidewalk.

I walk up to the building. Two kids are already checking my car out. I hail them. They walk over, looking ready to run or try to knife me. "You want to earn fifty bucks?" I say to them.

"Sure we do," the taller one replies like he's not earned that much in his life. "What d'ya need?"

"Watch my car while I'm in there. I come out and it's still there, you get paid. Deal?"

"How do we know you'll pay up?"

"You heard of Marco Alessi?"

"Sure we have."

"That's me."

The shorter one sticks out a hand and shakes mine, his face solemn. They stand guard by the car while I walk into the building. The main door is hanging loose on its hinges.

I can see it once had a security system, but it looks like decades since it was last working. Same with the elevators. The button does nothing. Stairwell it is then. Smells of piss in here but I've worked worse places before.

Esposito owns this building. He's got about sixty percent of this district and he's run it down so much there's little money left in it. I'm not sure whether he's running some long game or just doesn't give a shit. As long as the drugs keep moving and buyers keep paying, he's happy.

The building's fucked and so am I if his people spot me here. I've no soldiers backing me up. Just me and my gun. I'm not scared. I'm prepared. Ready to do whatever I need to in order to get her out of here.

I reach her floor and step out onto shredded carpet that was once red. The walls are stained and covered in mold. The first door I pass, I hear the snoring of the doped on the other side. Next to that one, two people yelling at each other. I move on and then I reach her door. I listen. No sounds coming from inside.

I try the handle, slowly. It doesn't move. Locked. At least she's got some sense of danger. Not enough though or she wouldn't live in a shithole like this. No more moldy walls and yelling neighbors after tonight. No more broken windows and graffiti. She's going to be on the island with me. I'm going to treat her the way she deserves to be treated. Like a princess.

I pull out my lock picks and get to work, easing the two of them in and wriggling until I hit the sweet spots. Picking locks is like making women come. You just got to know how to line things up right. Nimble fingers help.

With a quiet click, I'm in. I ease the door open and then move silently inside. My heart sinks. She lives here? The place stinks of damp. She's got hardly any possessions. Bed with a lumpy mattress and one blanket. Freezing cold. A bookcase with a backpack on it. Books piled up next to it. I know she's a student so the notepads make sense but where's the food?

There's hardly anything in the refrigerator. Just milk and a cube of cheese a size I wouldn't leave out for a mouse. The cupboards are just as bad. Lemonade, the cheap stuff. Half a bottle of gut-rot whiskey. A sofa that looks like it could collapse into dust any second. A TV that's older than the building. That's it.

She's not here. I'm not sure where she is but I get a feeling she'll be back soon. I better move fast. I find a suitcase in her wardrobe and cram her clothes into it. I open her bedside drawer and there's a vibrator. I bring it.

The vibrator in my hand makes me think of her using it and my cock twitches at the memory of her climaxing.

I gather up her notepads and books and put them into

the case as well. She doesn't have anything else. I zip up the case, wheel it out the door, pulling it closed but not bothering to lock it.

I take the case down to the car. The boys are still standing guard so I give them a hundred each. "Thanks mister," they say in unison.

I'm about to tell them the job's not done yet when my cellphone buzzes in my pocket. I pull it out just as a car comes around the corner. "Scram," I tell the kids who are already vanishing into the distance. I get a bad feeling about that car. This is Esposito's district and the kids are running before I tell them. They probably called him. Told him I was here.

I answer the phone and it's Ben. "She's come back," he says. "Got her locked up safe."

I hang up just in time. The car is screeching forward, windows rolling down. I throw myself to the ground as they open fire. They don't slow down for a second but they're amateurs.

The driver is shooting when he should be watching the road. The passenger in the back is the one spitting most bullets at me.

The windows on the Ford shatter but they're aiming too high. I've my gun out but by the time I lean around the Ford to aim, they're already done for.

The driver didn't see the hydrant until he hit it and he slammed into it too fast to ever move again. The engine's done for. They've crashed and are clearly hurting. Badly.

I walk over, gun out. The two doors swing open and they try to get out but I put two shots in the passenger before he can even raise his gun at me.

The driver is coughing up blood, the steering wheel got him in the chest and he wasn't wearing his seatbelt.

His head's left a cobweb on the windshield. He looks up at me with one good eye, the other one swollen shut already. "Please," he begs. "Help me, I need an ambulance."

"I'll call the morgue," I reply, putting one between his eyes. I walk back to my car and put the suitcase in the trunk. Then I brush the glass off the driver's seat and climb in. I drive out of there slow and steady, sirens approaching in the distance. By the time the police tear past me I'm just one more car on the road.

I get out of the city with no more trouble. I don't know for sure if the kids called Esposito or he's been watching her place but either way I'm glad I'm out of there. I'm not going back until it's time to deal with him. That won't be long but first I've got to get back.

I have a woman in need of punishment.

I get to the dock and put the car in neutral. I get her case out the way and then push the trunk. The car rolls forward and splashes straight into the water, slowly sinking from view.

This way I can't be traced to the two dead men. I pay Gianni good money to make sure the cameras here never catch sight of me. I'm in a blind spot and glad of it more than ever today.

I get back into my boat and head for the island. I can take a good guess what happened. She went to give him the painting, and he told her it was fake, told her to go get the original.

I'm not letting her leave again. She's mine now. I own her.

The water's fine, and it doesn't take me long to get home. I tie up my boat next to hers and then step onto the dock. I walk back to the house carrying her case. It contains everything she owns in the world. There's no need for her to ever leave here again.

I warned her not to come back. I tried to tell her what would happen if I saw her again. This is on her. She had a choice. She chose to come back into my world. I'm glad she did. Means I get to see that sweet little ass of hers every single day for the rest of my life.

I get to the house and Ben's in the kitchen, making supper for him and Horace. "Talk to me," I say as I walk in.

"Just like you predicted. She triggered the dock alarm and then ten minutes later came in through the window you left open. We were waiting on the other side and grabbed her before she got two feet inside."

"She give you any trouble?"

"Kicked like hell and bit Horace on the arm. Cursed us a bit but nothing we can't handle."

Horace looks up at me. "Maybe you should make a deal with Esposito."

I frown at him. "Where the fuck did that come from?"

"I'm getting too old to be chasing down assassins. One of these days he might send enough people to do some actual damage. What's the harm in negotiating?"

"I'm going to pretend you didn't say that. She eaten anything?"

"Not yet," Ben answers. "I was just going to take this up to her."

"I'll do it. You go scuttle her boat. Make sure it goes down where no one will ever find it."

"You got it boss. Should I start setting the table for two each night?"

"We'll see." I take the tray. It's got a sandwich, tuna on rye. Glass of milk. Candy bar and banana. Everything she needs to see her through tonight.

I head upstairs, carrying the tray in one hand, and her suitcase in the other. I stop outside her new bedroom. It's next to the red room, the punishment room, but she doesn't know about that yet.

I take a deep breath and then unlock the door.

It's time to inform my new guest of the house rules.

FIFTEEN

ELLIE

I can't believe I let it happen. For the second time in as many days I'm tied to a bed in Marco Alessi's house. The first time I could blame circumstances. This time? It's my fault. I can't blame anyone else but me.

I thought I was doing so well. I brought the boat into the harbor and there was no sign of him. I waited for ages and still no sign. Only when I was certain that there was no one there did I make my move.

I kept to the treeline all the way to the house, not once stepping out into the open. I made it without being seen, climbed through the first open window I saw and dropped straight into the arms of his two servants. I fought like a wounded animal but they were too strong for me.

Now I'm here, tied down to a bed again. Not a four poster this time. Up on the second floor. Still got ropes attached to the corners though, digging into my wrists and ankles.

I'm dressed where I was only in towels last time. Maybe I should be grateful for small mercies.

I've no idea what he's going to do to me when he gets here but I can take a good guess. He's not going to be happy, that's for sure.

I don't know how long I'm laid on my back for but when the bedroom door is unlocked, I'm almost grateful. I can't escape these ropes on my own without tearing all the skin off my wrists. They're bound too tightly.

It was such a simple job. Get the painting. Get my sister back. Have nothing to do with Marco Alessi ever again. I failed completely.

He walks in carrying a tray in one hand and a suitcase in the other. I get a horrible feeling the case is for me to go inside, chopped into pieces. "I told you not to come back," he says, setting the tray down next to the bed. I look at it, wondering if I'm going to see syringes and scalpels. I breathe an audible sigh of relief when I find myself looking at a sandwich and a glass of milk.

"Let me go," I tell him.

He shakes his head, reaching into his pocket. He brings out a large handkerchief which he wraps around my flailing head. He ties it tightly into a gag, leaving me unable to say anything. I can taste the cloth and I start to panic, fighting the bonds until they're digging into my skin. "Most people who refuse to follow my instructions, do you know what happens to them?"

I glare up at him, cursing as loudly as I can into the gag.

"I kill them." He says it in a conversational tone, as if he's talking about the weather. "Want to know why you're not dead?"

He picks up the glass of milk and examines it before setting it down again. "If you promise to behave, you can have something to eat and drink. How does that sound?"

I continue cursing but he doesn't seem in the slightest

bit bothered, continuing his speech. "You came back here. I'm guessing you came for the real painting. This time you're staying until I give permission for you to leave. I can tell I'll have my work cut out so be warned I will keep a close eye on you. Obey me and all will be well. Fight me and you'll see how cruel I can be. Understand?"

I stop fighting. His eyes are boring into me and I'm like a rabbit in headlights. I can't do anything but look back at him. "Will you be good?" he asks.

I manage a slow nod. I don't mean it. First chance I get, I'm running for the boat. I haven't got time to mess around here with him. I've a deadline to meet.

"Good." He reaches down and unties the gag. "Be nice," he says, pointing a finger at me.

I take a rasping breath, scared by how shaky my voice sounds as I speak. "I need the painting," I tell him. "Otherwise Esposito's going to kill my sister."

His brow furrows but only for a moment. "What timeline?"

"What?"

"How long did he give you?"

"Forty-eight hours."

"Starting when?"

"I'm guessing from six. That's when the meeting was set up."

"You went to the meeting then? Did you see him in person?"

"Yeah, why?"

He sits on the edge of the bed, a strange smile flickering on the edge of his lips. "Because if you had talked to me first, I could have killed him there and then. Get me close to him, I can kill him." He strokes his chin. "I'm going to offer you a deal. I give you the painting. You make sure he

95

comes to you personally to collect it and I'll take care of the rest."

"But what about Christine?"

"I'll guarantee she'll be safe, don't worry about that. What do you say? Do we have an agreement?"

I think for a moment. I like the idea of Esposito dead. That way he can't come back to bite Christine on the ass. "What if he finds out you're coming for him?"

"Won't matter. He's only got eyes for the painting. He won't be able to focus on anything else until it's too late."

"What's so special about this painting anyway?"

"It belonged to my father. He had a master forger working for him back then. I don't know if you know this but oil paint, when it's dried, can be lifted off the canvas if you have someone who knows what they're doing. Got a section of paint lifted just enough to write the number of a Swiss bank account down there. Esposito wants what's in that account."

"Who does it belong to? The money, I mean."

"Me. I inherited it."

"So that's why he wants the painting? To steal your money?"

"He stole the painting back when I was a kid. It was useless to him because all he knew back then was my inheritance was in the painting. Thought it meant how much it would sell for at auction. Only found out about the Swiss account from the forger once I'd got the painting back. He's been looking for it ever since and someone must have squealed for him to know it's right here on the island."

"And you're willing to give it to me?"

"I'm willing to trade it with you. You spend the next forty-eight hours with me. At the end of that time I give you the painting."

"Just like that?"

"Just like that." He puts a hand out to stroke my leg. I try to yank it away even though the touch is comforting. I don't want to be comfortable around him. He's a killer. "Say yes and I might untie you."

"Might?"

"You'll have to earn things during your stay here. Be good and you'll earn the painting."

"And what if I'm not good?"

"The room next to this one is called the punishment room for a reason."

I shudder at the way he's looking at me. Like he wants to take me in there right now. "

"All right," I say, thinking that as soon as I'm free and can get hold of the painting I'm getting the hell out of here and not looking back. "How much is in that account?" I ask.

"Little over twelve million."

"Oh, that all?"

He doesn't seem to get the sarcasm. "The rest has been spread out in different places since then. Esposito thinks the whole fortune is still in there."

"So just how much are you worth if twelve million is only a small piece?"

"Enough to get by."

"So, do you own this island or lease it? Do you have to give it back at the end of the term?"

A rumbling laugh comes up out of his throat, sounding like he's not laughed in a long time. "I own it. Own everything on it as well. Including you."

"You don't own me."

"I do for the next two days. If you want the painting and want your sister back, that is."

"So you're happy to let my sister die if I don't do what you say?"

"What happens to her is none of my concern. That's on you. Think you can do what it takes to win her freedom?"

"I'd do anything for her."

"Then we have an agreement."

He stands up and taps the suitcase. "In here is everything I found in your apartment. Your clothes, though I have better things for you to wear. Your books, your toothbrush. It's all in there."

"You broke into my apartment?"

"I collected your things. Thought you would want them during your stay here."

"What gives you the right to do that?"

"A cat burglar criticizing someone for forced entry? That's rich. It's done. Accept it." He unzips the case and begins emptying things onto the chest of drawers near the fireplace. He picks up each book in turn and looks at the spine. "Wuthering Heights," he says, holding onto the last one. "You a fan?"

"It's required reading for my college course."

"I know."

"Is there anything you don't know about me?"

He crosses to the bed and opens the book at the bookmark, starting to read.

I listen. It's a surreal experience. I'm tied to his bed. I can't look at him without feeling arousal I don't want building inside me. But I can listen to him reading the story as his growl becomes warmer, more soulful. I find my eyes half closing as he continues.

When he gets to the end of the chapter he stops. "More later," he says, putting the book with the others. "It's time to begin your punishment for running away."

"Punishment? What punishment?"

"This is happening, Ellie. The sooner you accept it, the better." He reaches up to the ropes holding my wrists in place and unties them. "When these are removed you are going to stand up with your hands behind your back. You are going to face me and you will not speak until I give you permission. You will answer yes, Sir, or no, Sir, when I ask you a question. Is that clear?"

I look up at him, and I see he's serious. There's no other way of getting out of here but playing along until I have time to run. "Yes, sir."

He moves down to the ropes tying my ankles. Undoing the knots, he lifts one leg after the other, his hand warm and huge, the touch sending electricity through my body. "Up," he says. "Stand there." He points at a spot near the door. I could try to run but I don't have the painting yet.

That's what I tell myself when I stand with my hands behind my back, facing him as he said. I don't want to admit this is exciting. Submitting to him is doing things to me I didn't expect. The feeling scares me.

"Follow me," he says, opening the door and walking along the hall to the next room. He pushes the door open and steps aside. I walk in and gasp at the sight in front of me. Ropes, chains, restraints. A chair with a hole in the seat. Drawers containing who knows what. "Over there," he says. "Bend over the wooden horse."

It's one of those things you vault over in gym class. I lean over it and he grabs my wrists, tying them to the front side, leaving me trapped in place. Moving behind me, he reaches for the waistband of my sweatpants, dragging them down my hips, taking my panties with them. My ass comes into view and I try to free myself but I'm going nowhere, my wrists tightly bound once more.

"I will paddle you for running from here without permission," he says, still lowering my pants down to my ankles. I can feel his hot breath on the back of my legs. He must be so close to me. "For stealing the painting, I have something more serious in mind."

He walks around to the chest of drawers in front of me, sliding them open. He reaches inside and pulls out a tube of something. I'm not sure what it is but I work it out when he brings out a butt plug of solid steel. It has a jewelled base and looks expensive. "Ever had one of these inside you?" he asks.

"Please let me go," I say, fighting my bonds again. "I've changed my mind. I don't want to do this."

"I told you. You're mine for forty-eight hours. You will take your punishment. You will submit to me. Don't pretend you don't want to." He walks back over behind me, sliding a hand between my legs. "I can feel how wet you are," he says, his fingers slipping between my folds. "Why pretend otherwise?"

SIXTEEN

MARCO

"**P**lease," she says like begging will stop me. I've had people beg for their lives. I never listened. No mercy. "Please don't do this."

"You came back," I reply, applying lube to the tip of the plug, rubbing it along the surface with my fingers. I take my time, making sure she can see me. The anticipation makes it all the better. I know what's going to happen and so does she. "I warned you what would happen if I saw you again. You returned to steal something from me and instead I am going to steal your innocence from you."

She looks up into my eyes and something else replaces the fear, just for a moment. I know that look. I saw it in her eyes when we were in the restaurant together. It's curiosity. It's gnawing at her.

Despite herself she wants to know. It's overriding the nerves, the anxiety, everything negative. It's the spark I intend to blow upon until it becomes an all engulfing blaze. An inferno that heats us both up and creates something unique, something I can only get from her, from someone willing to fight me.

I know she'll submit eventually but to submit too easily? Who wants that? What would be the point of a football match where one side just stood there and did nothing? A hockey goalie who leaned on the net and closed his eyes. I want her to struggle. I want her to fight her own desire. I want to work through her neuroses about who she really is.

I know who she is even if she doesn't. She's my submissive. She's going nowhere until she admits it.

I finish applying lube to the plug, holding it in front of her face. "This is going in your ass and then me and you are going to eat supper together."

"Please, don't do this."

"Don't pretend you don't want this, Ellie." I walk around behind her and slide my fingers along her pussy, finding the burning hot hole in the center of her, the core where nothing can hide from me. I slip a finger into her, pushing it deep, adding a second, listening to her breathing as it changes. "Your body can't lie to me."

She lets out a moan as I thrust into her twice. "Please," she begins, but the strength has gone from her voice. She's muttering half words as I slide back and forth inside her.

"You like submitting to me," I tell her. "Let go of your fears and allow yourself to be my slave."

"But..." Her voice trails off.

"If you say another word, I will gag you and then you will eat nothing until tomorrow night. The plug will still go into you but you will be bound to this wooden horse and left unable to move until I see fit." I let my hand slide out of her and then up along the valley of her ass, my finger brushing her private little hole. "Not another word," I say in a growl.

I move my fingers around her asshole in a circle,

resisting the temptation to dip into her. Punishment first, then pleasure. She needs to know exactly who's in charge here and it's not her. It's me.

I take the tip of the plug and press it toward her ass. At the same moment I move my other hand between her legs and stroke her clit as softly as I can. She moans in response, shifting her hips in place. But when I nudge the plug forward I can see her buttocks tensing up. I move my fingers a little faster on her clit. "If you're good, I'll let you come for me. Wouldn't you like to come, Ellie?"

"Hmm hmm," she says, resisting saying anything out loud.

"Good girl," I reply. "You're learning fast." I continue stroking her clit, delving into her pussy now and then, feeling how wet she's become from this. "You know you need to be punished for lying about this. I know you want this as much as I do. I know you want to come as much as I want to see it. If you're good you'll have the best orgasms of your life while you're here. Now take a deep breath and take your punishment."

As she breathes in, I hold the plug in place. When she exhales, I push it firmly past the point of resistance. She gasps in shock but by then it's in her, the jewelled base sticking out, making me want to replace it with my cock. "Before you leave I'm going to come in your ass, Ellie. My cock will be deep inside there. I bet you're tight in there, aren't you?"

She almost answers. I hear the intake of breath and then the start of a word but then she stops herself. I move the plug around in a circle, my other hand still playing with her clit. "Would you like to come, Ellie?"

She says nothing but I can tell by her breathing that's exactly what she wants.

I move around the wooden horse so she can see me. I lift her chin so she's looking straight at me. "You come when I say so and you ask me permission every time. Is that clear?"

She looks like she's about to speak but then she nods. Her cheeks are flushed, her eyes wild. "You're learning," I tell her, walking over to the drawer and bringing out a paddle. "Half a dozen and then I will feed you."

She shakes her head but I ignore her, walking around the back of her and raising the paddle. "You must understand," I say as I hold it in the air. "I am a man who sees the world a certain way." I bring the paddle down so it smacks across her ass. She cries out as the sting spreads through her.

My cock springs forward in my pants at the sight of her reddened ass. "For every crime there is a punishment. For every sin, there is a penance." I bring the paddle down a second time. "You came to steal from me. You left my island without my permission. You refuse to admit you want to submit to me." I spank her ass again, harder this time. Her breathing is becoming ragged. I know she can't take much more. I land the final three blows slowly, leaving a tantalizing gap between each one. "You will."

Once I'm done, I return the paddle to the drawer and then bring out the after-spank cream. I apply a portion to my fingers in front of her, noting that her eyes are fixed on the bulge in my pants. "The punishment is over," I say. "The crime is forgiven. Now you can have a fresh start." I walk behind her and being applying the cream to her burning hot ass. "This will help with the pain." I slide my hand into the valley of her ass, loving the feel of her soft skin under the cream.

I want to fuck her more than anything but not yet. I do things in the right order. Never let pleasure impede business. This is business. "You hate me now," I say, moving my hand closer to her clit. "But by the time this is over, you will beg me to let you stay."

"Bullshit," she replies.

"That word has slipped out," I tell her. "But I can't let it go. What kind of man would I be to lay down rules and not enforce them? You will eat nothing this evening. The plug will remain in until I say otherwise. Such a shame you could not control yourself. I was about to let you come."

I pull her panties back up to her thighs. I reach between her legs again, finding her clit, teasing it gently, listening as her breathing changes again. I get her closer and closer to an orgasm. The moment I am sure she's about to tip over the edge, I stop, yanking her panties back down to her ankles. I walk around to untie her wrists. As I undo the knots I tell her how it's going to be from now on.

"You will remove your shoes and socks. You will keep your panties and pants around your ankles. You will get on your knees," I tell her. "You will crawl through to the bedroom and once there you will climb onto the bed, remaining on all fours. Is that clear?"

She nods, looking on the verge of tears. I like that frustrated look. All she wants in the world is to be allowed to climax but she broke a rule. She has to pay the price.

I finish untying her wrists, stepping back and pointing at the floor. She looks at me and swallows hard, rubbing where the bonds were on her arms. I think she might be about to defy me. For a brief moment, I am not sure if she will obey. It's only a moment but then I am certain again. Her eyes dip and she lowers herself onto all fours. "Good girl," I tell her, moving behind her. "Off you go."

I watch her ass as she crawls through to the bedroom. I can't take my eyes off it, especially the way the plug moves with each shift of her stance. I'm almost disappointed the journey isn't longer.

She gets into the bedroom and clambers onto the bed, remaining on all fours, knees tight together. Her pussy forms a shiny peach, the soft folds coated in wetness, glistening in the light. "Knees apart," I tell her.

She obeys at once. "Forty-eight hours," I tell her. "It will pass before you know it." I stroke between her legs again. "If you promise to be good, I will remove the plug before tying you down. Do you promise, Ellie? You can answer me."

"I promise," she says in a whisper.

"What do you promise?"

"I promise to be good, Sir."

"That's my girl. Keep still." I reach out and take hold of the plug, easing it out of her. There's a moment where it seems stuck. There always is. Then it comes free into my hand. "Reach behind you and pull your cheeks apart," I tell her. "Let me see that asshole of yours."

She does as I say at once. She's already becoming more obedient. I lean down, looking from her pussy to her asshole. "Any idea how perfect you look?" I ask. "So beautiful. If you behave overnight like you promised, I will let you come in the morning. You are not to touch yourself tonight. A camera will be watching. I will know if you do. Now into bed and I shall read to you some more."

She lets go of her ass but the sight remains long in my memory. She rolls onto her back and climbs straight under the covers. I shake my head at her. "We don't go to bed with our clothes on, do we?"

She looks at me and opens her mouth but I put a finger to my lips. "You will sleep naked while you are here. Take your clothes off and give them to me."

She rummages under the covers, trying her best to keep

the blanket over her. I take each item she passes me. Panties, pants, top, bra. I know she's naked under there and my cock throbs at the thought of whipping the blankets away and ravaging her. I want to so badly but I am a man of my word. "I will fuck you tomorrow," I tell her, folding her clothes neatly as I talk. "You will not come until I give you permission. If you are good, the rewards will be yours. If you misbehave, I might not let you leave here ever again."

I place the folded clothes on the floor by the bed. Then I pick up Wuthering Heights, perch myself on the bed beside her, and start to read. Her eyes sag almost at once. I'm not surprised. Submission can be tiring. By the time I reach the end of the chapter, she's fast asleep.

I lean down and kiss her forehead. That done, I close the book, pick up her clothes, and walk out with them. I lock the door behind me. She promised to behave but I'm no fool.

I know she's likely to try to escape again. I intend to make sure that doesn't happen. I flick the alarm on. The slightest hint of her fiddling with the door or window and I'll know.

I'll know, and I'll punish her for it.

I head for my own bedroom. It's time to get some rest. I have a long day ahead of me tomorrow.

SEVENTEEN
ELLIE

I don't know who I am anymore. I remember this one time a caterpillar decided to take up home in the corner of the prison yard. No one else had noticed it but me. I was sitting as far from the other inmates as I could get and it was crawling along like it was on a mission.

I sat watching as it climbed up the side of the wall until it got to the underside of a window ledge. Still no one else had seen it. It was just this black and white spiky furry thing and then it changed. I sat there and watched it make a chrysalis out of nowhere. It was like alchemy.

Every day during exercise time I thought someone would spot it and flick it away, snap it off and there would go the caterpillar.

I kept watching, trying to look like I wasn't looking. Then one day out of nowhere, it was gone. I never saw it emerge. I just saw the chrysalis peeled back, and I knew a butterfly had flown away, up out of the prison yard, disappearing to wherever it had to be.

I don't know what kind of butterfly it was but I do know

it came into the prison a caterpillar crawling along the ground and it left flying on its own wings. I like to think it was beautiful but I'll never know.

I feel like the caterpillar must have felt inside the chrysalis. I'm trapped in this room. The windows are barred, and the door is locked. There doesn't even seem to be a lock on this side for me to pick. I'm guessing he's bolted it on the outside, knowing I'm bound to try and escape.

I wake up in the morning, and I don't know who I am. I don't know what I am. A caterpillar? A butterfly? A criminal? A kidnapping victim?

I sit up and I can still feel the sting from where the paddle hit me. What does it say about me that I felt like I deserved it? That I deserved the pain? That it felt good at the deepest level inside me? Christine used to hit me when I was little and she's drag out arguments for days. He paddled me and that was it. Punishment over. So different. So much better.

I can still tell where the plug was. I'll be feeling it all day. What does it mean that when he said he would fuck my ass, I wanted him to do it?

I need to get a hold of myself. I need to not fall for whatever black magic he's using on me. There's something about him that is like more like alcohol than drugs. Just being in his presence gets me hammered. I get drunk on him, on the way he speaks, the way he acts. Everything about him changes me. It's only when I'm alone that I get the hangover from it all.

He kissed me last night.

He thought I was asleep. I was listening to him read and trying to forget everything that had just happened. He leaned down and kissed my forehead. I wanted so much more. I wanted him to stay. I almost said so but I managed to resist.

That's what I need to do. I need to resist him. I'm being held against my will. I'm only here for the painting. I need to get out of here as fast as I can. Not easy as he took my clothes last night.

I'm naked in bed and I feel a heaviness down in the pit of my stomach. No, lower than that. I know what it is. It's because I didn't get to come last night. This is why I don't know who I am. He tied to me to that wooden horse. He paddled me. He violated my ass with that steel plug.

He put two fingers inside me and brought me to the brink of orgasm against my will. I should hate him. I tell myself to hate him but I can't do it. I don't even know why. All I know is that I want to come more than anything. Memories of last night are washing over me.

My eyes close and my hands slide down under the blankets. I feel my nipples, both rock hard and super sensitive. I shift my hips, knowing what I want to do. An ache is growing down there and I could relieve it so easily. I searched through my suitcase and found my vibrator first thing this morning. I could use it.

I manage to stop myself. He might be watching me, he might not. I don't want to risk it. I don't want him any angrier than he already is.

You want to submit to him. You want to please him.

I don't know where that thought comes from but I don't like it. It's not true. I'm not doing this because I want to submit to him. All right, maybe I am but I can't. It's not right. He's keeping me prisoner. He's not heading anywhere near to getting consent from me.

You gave him your consent. You came back to him. You knew what he'd do to you.

"Shut up," I say to the voice in my head. I climb out of bed and wrap the blankets around me. I've already gotten up once, checking the window and the door. That was when it was still dark. It's daylight now.

The view outside is beautiful. The early sun is sparkling out on the water beyond the edge of the island. Nearer, I can see trees and birds circling them. Below me a lawn coated in dew. A blackbird is hopping across it.

"Good morning." His voice. Behind me.

I never even heard him unlock the door. I spin around so fast I almost drop the blankets. I scrabble for them and manage to keep myself covered. He's holding a silver tray with a cover hiding the contents. "Is that breakfast?" I ask, nodding toward the tray.

"Of sorts. Lay back on the bed and close your eyes."

"Why?"

"Because you have behaved and that means you get a reward."

"What's on the tray?"

"You'll never find out if you don't lay on your back and close your eyes."

I walk over to the bed and climb onto it, looking past him at the open door. "Don't even think about it," he says, reading my mind. "I hid the painting and I doubt you want to leave without it."

I lay back, head on my pillow, eyes closed. "What are you going to do to me?" I ask as I hear him walking closer.

"You'll see. If you open your eyes at any point, this stops and I leave."

"Why? Why can't I look? Are you going to hurt me?"

"I do not hurt. I only punish when you are bad."

"What's the difference?"

"Punishment is in response to a crime. Hurting is what sadists do to their victims."

"And you don't think I'm one of your victims?"

"You are my submissive and you will say nothing else until I give permission."

I feel something on my leg, down by the ankle. It's soft and gentle. I work out eventually that it's a feather. He flicks the blankets off me and I can feel his gaze on my body.

This is different to last night. It's like he's a different person. Gentler, softer, more caring. Does he know who he is? I find myself wondering. Maybe he's as lost as me.

The feather moves up my leg, and I shift my knees apart. I know he's looking at my pussy and I want him to stare. I want his eyes fixed on me. Right now I like being the object of his obsession. I spent so much of my life feeling powerless that it feels good to have this hold over someone so powerful. That's what this is. It brings me up to his level rather than bringing him down to mine.

The feather traces a line over my thigh and then between my legs. It brushes lightly over my clit and then moves up my stomach. I try to control my breathing but I know the slightest touch from his fingers and I'll come.

He circles my nipples, and I gasp when he suddenly takes the left one into his mouth. He sucks hard and then grazes it with his teeth, tugging slightly. The pain makes me wince, but it brings pleasure with it. All too soon I can only feel the feather, moving back down my body, bypassing my clit this time before disappearing.

There is a moment of silence. Nothing happens but I'm biting my lip with anticipation. I can hear clothes rustling. Is he getting undressed? I want to open my eyes but I dare not do it. I need to come and if I look at him, it won't happen. He's in charge of this moment. He's in charge of me. He's taken control of my very soul. I belong to him right now. I can think about what a bad idea this is later.

He's moving around the side of the bed, climbing up, straddling my chest, squashing my tits under his thighs. "Open your mouth," he says.

I know what's coming, but it's still a shock. "Tongue out," he adds.

The tip of his cock slides over my lips. It's huge and heavy and throbbing with heat. It pushes all the way to the back of my throat. Once it's there, he grabs my hair, holding me in place.

Drool is running down my chin. I can't swallow. I can't breathe. I can't do anything but be impaled by his shaft.

"You belong to me," he says. "You will open your mouth and swallow my cock whenever I command it. Do you understand?"

I muffle a reply around his shaft. "I'll take that as a yes," he says, thrusting. "Suck my cock, Ellie. Show me what you can do. Make me want to let you come."

My tongue moves automatically, sliding along the length of him, finding the tip, circling it quickly. All the while he keeps thrusting so I reach up and grab his length, marvelling at the size of it. I haven't even seen it yet, but it's in my mouth right now.

He's naked and I want to look at him but I don't dare to disobey. I reach up and bring him further into my throat, squeezing the base, fondling his balls with my other hand, wanting him to come, wanting to show him what I can do.

"Not yet," he says when he realizes how desperate I am. He pulls free and I take several gasping breaths.

I wipe my chin as he moves down the bed, crushing me under his bulk. "I'm going to come in you," he says. "Next time, I will make a mess of you but this first one, you will not spill a drop."

He leans down and presses his lips to mine. As he kisses me, I feel his cock digging into my stomach. It's twitching and my body is responding. The kiss deepens into an embrace, his tongue exploring my mouth. Do I taste of him? I've no idea but he doesn't seem to mind.

He shifts his hips as he stops kissing me, leaning up on his arms, moving so the tip of his cock is rubbing along my pussy. "You will ask me if you can come," he says, reaching down and guiding himself over my clit, drawing a light moan from me. "You will not come without permission."

He thrusts and I can't help but cry out. I almost climax just from that single thrust. It's not just the dull emptiness being filled and stretched more than any other man could. It's the way his pelvic bone rubs my clit in just the right way. He remains buried in me, driving deep, grinding his body against mine. "You can ask," he says. "Whenever you're ready."

"Please, let me come," I beg, shocked by how whiny my voice sounds. I'm clawing at his back, my whole body on fire. "Please, Sir. Please, let me come."

"You want to come with my cock in you?"

"God, yes."

I hear something being picked up from under the pillow. He presses it into my hand. "That's your bullet vibrator," he says, pulling back and slamming into me a single time. "I found it in your apartment. Show me how you use is. Show me how you like to come."

He moves my hand between my own legs. I've never masturbated in front of anyone before but with him it just happens. I find the button and hit it. The vibrations buzz to life at once and as I press it to my clit, I barely have to circle my nub thirty seconds before my climax is racing through me.

I contract around his cock, gripping him in place. He moves through the sensation, pulling back and slamming into me at full force, pounding into me without stopping.

The intensity of it all whips the breath from my body. My climax is still washing over me as he grunts and then drives all the way inside. His cock spurts into me. The sensation sends me over the edge for a second time. My body shakes in place as he collapses onto me. It's only for a moment, but I feel a connection to him that I've never felt with anyone.

Then the moment passes, and he's pulling out of me. I hear the rustling of clothes and then the door opening and closing. I look up but he's already gone.

I'm alone again.

EIGHTEEN
MARCO

I give it a couple of hours to make the arrangements. The time it takes gives me a chance to get a hold of myself. I need to. I can't believe what was going through my head.

Falling in love?

That's not something I do. It's not in my nature. I fuck women. I use them. I make them submit. I don't turn it into anything it's not. Love isn't in my nature. Yet, this morning, I could feel myself falling head over heels with her.

It was several tiny things and then one big thing. First, it was the way she responded to me. It was like I could see inside her head, see her fear about submission. She wanted to fight me. She wanted to lie, to pretend that wasn't who she was. I knew the truth already. She is built for this. She just needs to admit it.

Then there was the kiss. The way it felt when my mouth pressed against hers, like I wanted to claim her and never let her out of my sight. There's my usual obsessive nature but then there's this. This is new. This is so much more intense.

It's like I was looking at a mountain peak surrounded by clouds, certain I'd reached the top. Then we kissed, and the clouds parted and there's another peak above this one. I climbed higher than I've ever been, got closer to the summit I will never let myself reach. No mercy. Compassion is for the weak.

I can't care for her. Eventually she'll be gone. One way or another. In this life it's better not to get attached to anything. I can't believe I was thinking of having kids with her, being married to her. That's not happening. I'll fuck her. I'll turn her into a submissive. I might even keep her as a pet. But I will not love her. That is not who I am.

That's why I had to get out of there. I moved faster from the room than I ever would have planned. I plan everything but I didn't plan that.

That was the big thing. The instant we came together, our souls entwined. I'm sounding like I've come out of the book I was reading to her. Her influence is sinking into me and I can't allow that.

I can't fall for her. I'm a loner. I don't do relationships. I don't do love. Simple as that.

I got the hell out of there and I'm glad I did. I got in the shower and let it run ice cold, freezing my blood and my brain. When my mind settled I got myself a drink and got a hold of myself.

I'm me again now. Back to the way I've always been. In charge of my own head.

I will keep her. I will not get attached to her. I don't do attachment. You get attached, and you get taken advantage of. That's what happened before. It will not happen again. It will never happen again.

At noon I unlock the bedroom and walk back in. She's sitting up in bed, staring into space. She looks like she's been crying. I don't ask about it. I toss her a dress. "Put that on and be outside your room in five minutes."

She looks like she's about to say something but then she nods. I walk out and close the door, marking the time on my watch. Just looking at her made me want to drop all my barriers, run and comfort her, find out why she was crying and fix it. Make sure she never cries again. Fuck, I need to make sure I don't fall for her.

She's not going to love me back. I know that. Just wanting her to makes me vulnerable. I hate that. She's only here because of the painting. As soon as she has that, she's a ghost. She'll get hold of her sister and run. That's if Esposito lets her go.

I know him better. I know he'll never let her go. He's just using her to get the painting. That's why I need to kill him. End this war once and for all.

Got to be worth the gamble, right?

What's life without risk? Last time I was in Gordon's Cove for the night, I was in Gianni's casino, sliding all in on sixteen in blackjack. Dealer asked me if I was sure. That's what I said back then. What's life without risk?

Might have lost half a mil that night but I made it back soon enough. Deals between the families keep the money flowing. Except Esposito thinks he can just take over, run the nose powder all across the country. That and the human trafficking. I can't allow that. I have my limits. Like his nephew killing those kids. A line was crossed. There are consequences.

I open the door and Ellie's ready. The silver dress clings to her in all the right places. A hint of cleavage but not too much. Nipples visible through the fabric. I like that she's not asked for any underwear.

"Do I get to wear shoes?" she asks.

"This way," I tell her, walking ahead to the dressing room at the corner by the stairs. I open the door and point to the walk in closet at the back. "Take your pick."

She looks past me. "Holy shit," she says. "Why so many women's shoes? You got a fetish or something?"

"My Ellie gets choices," I reply. "Don't be long."

"Why? What's the rush?"

"We're going out for lunch."

"Out? Out where?"

"The city."

"You're kidding, right?"

I shake my head. "It's a test. I want to see if I can trust you. I need to be able to trust you, Ellie."

"You can trust me?"

"We'll see. You picked yet?"

She looks back over her shoulder. "Give a girl a minute, would you?"

I glance down at my watch. We've an hour until the reservation. That's not enough time to take the boat. I pull out my cellphone and call Ben. "What's up, boss?" he asks when he answers.

"Get the chopper ready."

"Sure thing."

Ellie turns around with a pair of killer red heels. "The chopper?" she asks. "As in a helicopter?"

"Don't want to miss our reservation."

"Are these okay?" she asks, holding up a pair of killer heels.

"Perfect. Follow me."

She puts them on and scurries after me like a good submissive. I walk out and around to the helipad. The rotors are already moving by the time we get there so I motion for her to duck her head as we climb inside. I get her strapped in and her headset attached and then I tap Ben on the shoulder.

He starts his routine and up we go. "Surprised your not flying me yourself," Ellie says, her voice coming through my headphones.

"I prefer to let someone else do the boring part," I reply. "Gives me more time to look up your dress."

She clamps her knees together. I resist laughing.

I get to see the journey through fresh eyes. Her eyes. She marvels at the view when we're out over the ocean like she's never seen it before, pointing at the waves, the boats, the oncoming shoreline. I tell her what she's looking at as we sweep over Gordon's Cove and keep moving further inland.

We get to the city in time for my reservation, landing at the private airfield nearest the restaurant. A car's waiting for us there and I climb in the back with her, putting one hand on her knee once we've set off moving. "What are you doing?" she hisses in my ear as I stroke my hand higher.

"Seeing how well you obey," I reply. I keep moving my fingers higher, listening to her breathing changing. I'm just starting to enjoy how tense she's getting when we arrive.

The car stops and I get out first, holding the door for her. Valerio is at the restaurant entrance, smiling my way. "Mr. Alessi," he says. "I have the top table ready for you. This must be your date. What a beautiful young lady. You make Mr. Alessi happy. I can tell. Nothing gets past Valerio. You know many people fall in love here. We are a romantic place, here at Valerio's."

"Just here for the food," I say, cutting him off before he tries to get the two of us married off. We go inside and I'm immediately greeted by half the tables in there. People start to rise but I wave them away. I'm not interested in talking to anyone but her. "You back, Marco?" Jonathan asks, getting to his feet and trying to shake my hand. "We need you back. Esposito's been-"

I hold up a hand, silencing him. "Not now."

"Of course, of course." He nods and sits again.

"Who was that?" Ellie asks. "I recognise him from somewhere."

"The mayor," I reply. "Always asking for favors."

"You know the mayor? You just told the mayor not now?" She shakes her head. "And he listened? He never listens to anyone."

I hold out a chair for her. She sits. Valerio passes her a menu as I sit down. "Drinks?" he asks. "Champagne?"

I nod in approval.

He smiles. "I bring nothing but the best for you, Mr. Alessi. Anything you need, you just ask me."

I look down at the menu and then up at Ellie. She's got her brow screwed up and I can tell she doesn't speak Italian. I take her menu from her. "We'll have two of your meatballs."

Valerio nods and walks off and once he's out of earshot, Ellie leans toward me and whispers, "Sounds painful."

"What does?"

"Having two of his meatballs. Does he not need them?"

I manage to keep a straight face but only just. She's cracking through my armor step by step and I'm not sure I like it. I decide the best thing to do is get on top of the situation. I reach under the table and stroke her leg again.

"What are you doing?" she asks.

"You are going to walk into the bathroom in two

minutes," I reply. "You're going to get on your knees and open your mouth, hands on your head. Got it?"

She turns red, swallowing as she glances around her. "Here?"

"Two minutes."

I lean back and enjoy her discomfort. I'm in charge again, not her. She's not getting through my armor. I will use her for my pleasure. I will not fall for her. I will never allow myself to be vulnerable like that.

When the time is up she walks away and I give her a minute before I follow. I walk over to the ladies' bathroom and push open the door. She's right there by the sinks, on her knees, mouth open. My cock is already hardening at the sight. I start to unzip my pants.

"What if someone comes in?" she asks.

"No one will," I reply. "They all saw me follow you in here." I pull my cock out and stroke it as I walk toward her. "Now, no more talking." I slap it onto her tongue, enjoying the way her eyes widen at the sight. She didn't get to see it this morning, and she's clearly taken by the size. I know it's big. I've been told often enough. I also know she can take it all. She's proved that once already.

I push myself straight to the back of her throat, grabbing her hair and not letting her move away. I keep thrusting without stopping. Her tongue is driving me wild, and it's not long before I'm on the edge. I want to stay where I am but I resist.

This is part of the test. I pull out at the very last second so the first jets splash her face. She jerks away but only from the shock of it. Her tongue remains sticking out and the rest lands in her mouth. I squeeze my shaft, stroking it fast, making sure not to waste a drop. I slide to the back of her throat again.

"Clean me," I tell her. She brings her hands up and her tongue circles the tip in just the right way. When I'm satisfied I step back and hold out a hand, lifting her to her feet. "You are not to clean that off until we are sitting at our table," I tell her.

She runs a finger up to her face, feeling the edge of the mess I've made on her. "You're not serious. Are you?"

I take her hand and lead her out of the bathroom before she can say anything else. She fights me but only for a moment. Then she follows and we walk back to our table. The food is there ready for us. I tuck in. I'm hungry.

NINETEEN

ELLIE

I feel like everyone in the restaurant must know what happened.

I walk out of the bathroom and my cheeks are still hot and wet. I glance nervously around me but no one is looking our way. They're all busy talking, their attention elsewhere. I scurry after Marco and by the time I reach our table he's already started eating. He couldn't look more relaxed.

Me? I feel more on edge than ever.

I want to wipe my face but I can't. He hasn't given me permission yet.

A part of me loves the naughtiness of this moment. It's something I would never think of doing with anyone else. Somehow with him, it's all right. It's permitted. He's allowing me to be the kind of person I never knew I wanted to be. A submissive.

His submissive.

I look across at him, and he's picking up his napkin. He leans over and dabs at my cheeks with it. "You got something on you there," he says, cleaning me up more gently than I thought him capable of doing. "Made quite a mess on your face." Once he's done, he nods toward my plate. "Eat up. You must be hungry."

I pick at my food but my stomach's churning too much for me to want to eat much of anything. He seems unfazed by everything that's going on but I'm not sure I can cope with all this.

The worst part of it all?

I love it.

I loved every single moment in the bathroom just now. I loved choking on his length, kneeling and waiting for him to appear, knowing that all he was thinking about was me. It's a good feeling. Shit, that better not mean what I think it might mean.

Am I falling for him?

I can't fall for him. I can't love someone as cruel and cold as him. He's a killer and I'm an ex-con trying to go straight. I'm a student. I'm a loser. I'm not wife material. I'm not even lover material. I know he's just toying with me for fun.

Doesn't stop me wishing there was something more to this though.

Could there be? Is that possible? I jab at the salad on my plate, glancing up at him from time to time. I wish I could tell what was in his mind. This morning it felt like we had a real honest connection. Then he came and just got up and walked out the bedroom. Couldn't have made me feel more used.

But now this? Trusting me enough to come back to the city. He must know I could get up and walk out of here any time. Shout that I've been kidnapped by him, that I'm being held against my will. I could run out that door. There's nothing to stop me.

Yes, there is.

I need the painting. It's not just that though that is a big part of why I'm staying. It's also because I don't want this to end. The longer I spend with him, the more important I'm feeling. Like I actually matter in this world, that I have some significance.

My life has always felt like a waste but with him, I genuinely see a future for myself. One with a husband and with children. Me as his submissive for the rest of my life. How good would that be?

It's insane to even think about it. He held me against my will. He didn't listen when I told him to let me go. He's already done things to me that have caused me pain, that have bruised me. I only have to shift in my seat to be reminded of the paddling I endured at his hand.

Liked it though, didn't you?

I don't like that voice. I don't like the way it keeps cutting to the chase, cutting through my carefully honed defenses. I need those defenses. They've protected me all my life. I will not listen to that voice. I will not fall in love with a man who is so cold, so mercurial, so indifferent to my opinion.

"Let's take a drive," he says out of nowhere, tossing his cutlery onto his plate. "You don't look like you're ever going to finish that."

I'm glad to go. I'm glad to be in the car, away from all the people. I can't help feeling judged by them. Do they know what we did in there? Did they see what was on my cheek? Could they tell I liked walking through the restaurant like that? Could they tell a part of me wanted all their eyes on me, wanted to be the center of attention?

"Where are we going?" I ask as we get into the car.

"You'll see."

The driver seems to know where we're going. We take one turn after another. Marco is looking out the window but his hand's on my knee the entire time. I will it to go higher but he doesn't read my mind. I shift in my seat and move my knees slightly apart but he never moves an inch.

In the end I look out the window too in time to realize where we are. "That's my place," I say as the apartment disappears into the distance behind us. "Where are we going?"

"Wait and see." He says it without even looking at me.

We turn another corner and there's the library. The car comes to a stop by the entrance and Marco is out a second later, holding my door open. I climb out and he's taking something from the driver. It's the books I've been using for my course.

"What's going on?" I ask. I get the sinking feeling he's going to tell me I'm not allowed to study anymore. That would be just typical of a man like him. Wants his woman nice and tied down with no outside interests.

He walks up the steps to the library. Halfway up the two douchebags from the gas station are sitting there, legs splayed out, paper bags and whiskey bottles on the steps beside them. "Hey," Craterface says. "It's our little friend. Come sit with us."

Greasyhair grins, making obscene gestures with his hands.

"Friends of yours?" Marco asks.

"No," I reply bluntly. "Very much no."

"Who the fuck's that?" Craterface asks, too drunk to realize Marco is dangerous. "Got yourself a pimp, have you?

Told you our boss would hire you. He'll pay you a better percentage too."

Marco storms over to the two of them, towering over them. I'm scared on their behalf. I know what Marco did to Sergio back on the island. I saw the blood. "What the fuck do you want?" Craterface asks. Greasyhair is tapping his shoulder, his face pale. He's worked out who Marco is. Craterface is still hurling abuse. "Get the fuck out of here before I knife you."

Marco doesn't say anything. He leans down, grabs Craterface by the throat and lifts him up into the air, dangling him down as his face starts to turn purple, his legs lashing out but to no effect. "You speak to her again and I'll snap your neck," he says. "Got it?"

"Put him down," I shout. "Marco, you're killing him."

Craterface is gasping for air, his eyes bulging.

"Please, Marco. Let him go."

Marco drops him onto the step. "Compassion is for the weak," he says, looking back over his shoulder at me. "He insulted you. He should pay the price."

All the while, Craterface is gesturing at Greasyhair who finally gets it and pulls out a switchblade.

"Look out!" I shout to Marco but he's already noticed. He doesn't look scared. He's smiling back at the guy.

"Take your best shot," Marco says, his voice cold. "Go for it."

Greasyhair looks nervous, like he isn't used to this kind of reaction to his blade. He's used to people running, not smiling. He swipes it through the air but Marco moves so fast I can hardly tell what's happening.

All I see is his arm and hand whipping toward the knife and then all of a sudden he's holding it and the two drunks are running off down the steps, not looking back. Marco flips the knife into the air, catches it and then puts it in his jacket pocket. "Shall we?" he asks, turning to face me.

"Shall we what?"

"You have library books due back today. You need to renew them."

"Hang on. That's why we're here? For me to renew my library books?"

"Why else?"

He walks up the steps and pushes the door open, disappearing inside. I follow him, glancing over my shoulder in case Craterface and his chum decide to come back. I have to admit it. Seeing the way Marco handled them should have scared me but it didn't. It turned me on. Just one more thing for me to try to erase from my mind among so many others.

I find Marco at the desk inside and I join him in time for Mrs. Henry to finish stamping my books. "Friend of yours?" she asks, looking past Marco at me.

"Showing him the place," I reply. "Thought I might take him up to the top floor, look at the city."

She smiles. "Always nice to see a new face in here. Let me know if you need anything."

"Why do you look pissed off?" Marco asks as I walk over to the elevator. "You want to pay the fine for them if they're late? Could be down a whole dollar fifty."

"She thinks you're my boyfriend. She thinks I brought you in here to show you off to her, prove I have a man in my life."

"Do you think you have a man in your life?" The elevator doors open and we walk in together. I don't look at him while we travel up. I'm trying not to think about how I felt last time I was here. Horny as all hell and with no one to help me out. Not anymore.

Maybe I could take the initiative here. No, who am I kidding? That's not me. Not who I am at all.

"Definitely not."

"You sure?"

I want to tell him I do want him in my life but he's smiling that arrogant smile and I'm determined to wipe it off his face. "I'm sure."

The bell pings. I step out on the top floor and walk over to my usual spot. I'm not even sure why I've come here. My feet just did their thing without me really thinking about it. I turn around and Marco is right in front of me. "I see why you like it," he says, looking around him, sliding a book off the nearest shelf. "Titans of English literature and a decent view of the city. Oliver Twist. One of my favorites."

"You read Dickens?"

"Bill Sykes is my hero."

"Pretty sure he's the villain in that one."

"Must be why I like him. Oliver Reed played him well in the movie."

"He killed his lover."

"Oliver Reed?"

"Bill Sykes." I look at him, and his eyes are flashing light. "You're teasing me," I say, shoving him in the shoulder. "I believed you!"

"Shouldn't believe everything you hear. How come we're the only ones in here?"

"Rundown library in a bad part of town. Not exactly top of the popularity list. They had to shut the children's' reading corner last month. Budget cuts from the mayor's office. No one gives a shit about libraries anymore. Mrs. Henry's trying to raise funds to get it going again but no one cares about a dying library."

"So why do you come here?"

"Because it's near where I live and it has Internet access for my course."

"I'm impressed you're taking a college course, Ellie."

"You are?"

"It takes guts to change yourself. To make something of yourself. I'm proud of you for taking on the course."

"So you don't think I should quit?"

"What makes you say that?"

"Thought that's why you brought me here, to give the books back."

He shakes his head, frowning at me. "What kind of asshole do you think I am?"

"The kind that keeps women captive."

"You feel captive right now?"

"Well, not exactly but-"

"But nothing. You have choices to make, Ellie, same as all of us. When this is over, I'm hoping you choose to come back to the island with me."

"And if I don't?"

He gets even closer. "I'm going to make you come," he says, lifting me up and sitting me on the desk behind me. "Right now."

"What are you talking about? This is a public place. We were talking!"

"You said it yourself. Hardly anyone comes here. I already checked the whole floor. We're alone."

"Don't," I say, slapping his hands away as they slide up my dress. "Someone could see."

"Then we better be quick." He pushes my knees apart, lowering himself to the floor. He kneels before me, pulling my hips forward until my legs are dangling around his shoulders. He takes one look up at me. "You better not scream," he adds, pressing his lips to my pussy. "Might give the game away." His tongue dives straight into me and I gasp at the suddenness of it.

I clamp my hands to my mouth to keep quiet. One moment I'm about to demand that he stop. The next I don't want him to ever stop.

He knows exactly what he's doing with his tongue, sliding it up and over my clit, using his fingers to spread me wide. I'm already wet just from the way he's touching me. Soon I'm soaking.

I lower myself onto my back, closing my eyes and hoping Mrs. Henry doesn't come re-shelving up here anytime soon.

The tip of his tongue flicks over my clit, one finger plunging into me. The other hand is moving lower, finding my ass, using my own wetness to lube that hole. "I will not stop until you come for me," he says, sliding a finger an inch into my ass.

I feel fuller than ever before with fingers in both holes.

He moves them all in a perfect rhythm, one in, the other out, never stopping, only slowing or speeding up as the time passes.

I feel myself getting closer. The fact we're doing it here in public makes it all the more exciting. I can see the city through the window. Can it see me?

I reach down and run my hands through his hair, shifting in place as I bite my lip, knowing I'm right on the edge.

His tongue moves around my folds, teasing me briefly before returning to my clit, circling it faster this time. His mouth surrounds it, his lips on the core of me, tipping me over the edge as he thrusts his fingers deep into my pussy and my ass in the same moment.

I can't hold back any longer. My whole body shakes as

an orgasm rips through me. I have to put both hands over my mouth to stifle my cries of pleasure. Throughout, he continues to lick me, gentler now, so softly it doesn't overdo it as my climax fades.

I'm super sensitive down there and he seems to know that, easing his fingers from me slowly as the contractions in my pussy finally fade away.

"Good girl," he says, tugging my dress back into place as I hear the ping of the elevator over in the corner. I get up onto my feet, feeling dazed. I plaster a neutral expression my face as Mrs. Henry appears, carrying an armful of books. "You find everything you needed?" she asks.

"Definitely," Marco replies for me, reaching into his pocket and pulling out his wallet. He brings out a wad of banknotes and presses them into Mrs. Henry's palm.

"What's this for?" she asks, looking down at the money.

"A donation. Get the children's reading corner going again."

"I can't take this. It's too much."

"Marco takes my hand in his and leads me back over to the elevator, ignoring Mrs. Henry's attempts to give the money back.

We step into the elevator and the doors close. "How much did you give her?" I ask.

"Not much, just what I had on me."

"How much?"

"I've no idea."

"You must have a clue."

"Couple of thousand at most."

"You did that for me, didn't you? To try to impress me."

He turns and shakes his head. "Children need books," he says.

I look at him and at how earnest yet sad he looks. Before

I know what I'm doing, I'm kissing him. He looks surprised for a moment but then he's plunging his tongue into my mouth, claiming me with his body, his hands reaching up under my dress, squeezing my ass so roughly it hurts.

I melt into his arms, my body heating up.

All too soon the elevator doors are opening and we're walking out, my hand in his, acting as if nothing happened.

TWENTY

MARCO

I see the gun before it fires. We get outside, and my eye is drawn to the far side of the street. There they are. I'm lucky they're too angry to aim straight.

Ellie's behind me which makes life easier. I can protect her that way. We're walking out of the library and have barely begun walking down the steps. I have half a second to react, just enough time to shield her with my body.

The shot fires, hitting the stone wall beside the door. Chips of plaster fly off and catch the side of my face. I'm already reaching for my own weapon. I identify the shooters an instant later. It's those two assholes who were sitting on the steps when we went in.

I shouldn't have listened to her. I was about to choke the first one to death when she told me to put him down. I did it. What's wrong with me? I listened to her when I shouldn't and this is the result. You can't ever show mercy. People take advantage.

I pull out my pistol and flick the safety off in one motion. Then I'm shoving her back through the door and sinking to my knees. Another shot fires at me but this one's even wider of the mark. They're already shitting themselves.

I can see the two of them perfectly. People are scattering but my eyes are fixed on them. "Get out of sight," I tell Ellie as I squeeze the trigger. Craterface goes down. He was the one holding the gun. His friend scrambles for it in the dirt.

I'm running down the steps toward him, firing as I go. He's in the process of swinging the gun up to point at me when I get him. He's fumbling with the grip when my bullet smacks him in the middle of the forehead. He goes straight down, blood splattering behind him.

I don't hesitate. I cross the street and get to the two of them, firing one extra shot into each skull, to be sure. Then I get on the phone. "Ben," I say down the line. "Get me a clean up crew. North Street, opposite the library. Make it fast."

"Got it." He hangs up. I run back to the library. We need to make a move. There are witnesses who will be giving statements within a couple of minutes but the investigation won't go anywhere. My famiglia have enough people bought to make sure my name never gets anywhere near a charge sheet.

It's not like anyone's going to cry over these two. Scumbags who talk to her like that deserve everything they get. She's mine now. Try to hurt her and I'll make sure you pay the price.

I find her just inside the library door, not looking anywhere near as afraid as I expected.

"What happened?" she asks. "Did they hurt you?"

What a question. Bullets flying and her first thought is to worry about me. Maybe she does have feelings for me. I take her hand in mine. "Is there a back way out of here?"

"This way. Fire exit by the toilets." She leads me this

time and I follow, glancing back over my shoulder. I can hear sirens getting closer. Ben better not fuck this up. He needs to make sure the bodies are gone before the police arrive. That makes it much easier to sweep everything under the rug. Two bodies in a morgue and someone might ask questions. It might reach the Feds. No bodies and conflicting witness statements and we're home clear.

"Who were they?" I ask. "Anyone going to miss them?"

"I don't know their names. What happened out there? Where are they?"

"Dead."

"You shot them, didn't you?"

I push the fire exit open with my hip. "Are you going to tell me I should have let them go?"

"No." She sighs. "I'm glad they're dead. They've tried to touch me up in the past."

Jealousy and anger flare up in me. I want them alive so I can kill them again. Tried to touch her up? My girl!

"You should have let me choke him to death first time around," I say as we walk down the alley behind the library and out onto the next street. The sirens are getting louder. "We'll go back to the island for now. Let this die down."

"Hang on, are you saying you're going back on our deal?"

"I have you until tomorrow evening. Then you're back in this world with no one to protect you. Is that what you really want, Ellie? To be alone?"

"I won't be alone. I'll have my sister."

"If Esposito keeps his side of the bargain. Which he won't. I'm telling you right now, Ellie. The only way out of this is to work with me."

"With you? You just killed two men in the middle of the street."

"Men who were going to kill me. And once I was dead do you think they'd let you just walk away?"

She goes quiet for a minute. "Say I was going to work with you," she says after a while. "What would that entail, exactly?"

"You arrange your meeting with Esposito as planned. Lead me to him. I'll do the rest."

"You mean kill him."

"That's exactly what I mean. It's the only way you and your sister will be safe."

"If you come in with all guns blazing, she'll end up dead. I have to go alone."

"You can't do that. He'll never let you go."

"We made a deal. He'll honor it."

"Why would you trust him?"

She looks at me and all the warmth has gone from her face. "What choice do I have?"

"Let me do this my way. I take him out and everyone is safe."

She nods like she just worked something out. "That's why you're on the island, isn't it? You're afraid of him."

"I'm not afraid of anything."

"Then tell me how you really feel about me."

She looks at me, and I almost do it. "Come on, the chopper's around the next corner."

Ben's still off dealing with the clean up crew so I fly us back.

Maybe she's right. Maybe there is one thing I'm afraid of. Admitting how I feel about her. Even if I do kill Esposito, there are other families, other associates who might want to take out my woman.

If I bring her in, I can't stay on the island alone anymore. I'll need my support network around me. A lone wolf can get picked off easily enough but a pack of them? Never going to happen. Especially when they're all armed to the teeth and on their guard twenty-four hours a day.

I fly us back to the island and by the time we land, I'm thinking maybe this is the way to do it. Deal with Esposito, get her sister back. Then move off the island back to the city. Get back in charge.

I can't do anything about the two kids that died except wipe out the family name of the scumbag that shot them. Elda is dead. Kill his uncle, Lorenzo Esposito. Problem solved.

The only question is how do I get close enough to the most protected man in the city?

That's where she comes in.

There's a risk of course. A risk she could get caught in the middle of a shootout. She's already been in one while she's been under my protection. I'll have to make sure I get her to safety before the guns come out.

We land and get into the house. I leave her in the lounge and go make us some coffee. She's not there when I get back. I think she's run but I find her in my study, standing by the bookcase, scanning the shelves. She doesn't seem interested in *Girl in Chair*, behind the desk. I put the real one up there this time. She's barely glanced at it.

It's like she's forgotten what she came here for. "Lot of old English stuff here," she says, pulling one book out. "Is this a first edition?"

"They all are."

"So you're telling me this is the first edition of Wuthering Heights?"

"Use it instead of your library book. We left that behind."

"Yeah, right. Like I can underline bits of this."

"You can do what you want with it. I'm giving you permission."

"I shouldn't even touch it without gloves on."

"Books are supposed to be read, Ellie. They're not museum pieces."

"This one is. Fucking hell, this one too. And what's this? A first edition of The Odyssey?"

I frown but she winks as she turns around. "Just kidding."

"I know. The Greek first editions are on the second floor."

"Ha ha. You know, I never would have had you down as a literature fan."

"Movie buff too."

"Really?"

"You know nothing about me, Ellie. Put the book down and sit there. We need to talk."

She slides the book on the shelf like she's giving away her firstborn child. She gives it a last pat before coming to sit on the couch. I pass her a mug of coffee and then drag over an armchair. "Compassion gets you killed," I tell her. "Those guys shot at us because you wanted to be kind to them. You can't afford to be kind to anyone in this world, Ellie."

"Bullshit," she snaps straight back. "That's absolute bull-shit. What's the point of being alive if you can't be kind to people?"

"You get to stay alive."

"You saying you've done nothing kind in your life?"

"I've never shown compassion to men who insulted me."

"I've insulted you plenty. You've shown compassion to me."

"That's different."

"You just don't want to admit you've got a soft side but

I've already seen it. Shake your head all you like, I know it's there. Saw it when you were reading to me last night. Saw it at the library. You gave Mrs. Henry a shitload of money. When those guys fired, your first thought was to protect me, get me back inside to safety. That's compassion. That's kindness."

"You are a business asset. I protect my assets. That's all."

"Yeah well if you want to keep hold of this asset, you better start making better coffee. This is awful."

I shrug. "Too strong for you?"

"Needs sugar. A lot of sugar."

"Noted." My cellphone rings. I dig it out and get to my feet, walking out into the corridor.

"It's done," Ben says down the line but his voice sounds off.

"What is it? What's wrong?"

"They were associates of Esposito's. Low level pushers but still connected. He will not be happy if he finds out you whacked two of his guys on top of the three that came to the island."

I hang up. This could benefit me. Gives me an excuse to meet with Esposito. Pretend I'm there to apologize for killing his men.

I make calls. It's time to put a crew together. Time to end this once and for all. By the time I'm done, I'm ready to tell Ellie the plan. I walk back into the study, but I've been duped. I can't believe it. She's gone and so's the painting.

I go over to the open window and there's another open window on the far side of the courtyard. I can't believe I trusted her. She was just biding her time, waiting for an opportunity to get the painting. I was a fool to think she'd forgotten about it.

I'm going to have to move fast. She'll get to the boat

before I can but the helicopter's still out there. It needs fuel before I can take off though. I could run after her but she'll already be in my boat by now. I sank hers.

I'm an idiot for thinking I could trust her.

I know what's going to happen. She's going to Esposito and he's going to keep the painting and her. Or kill her when he finds out what I did at the library. Or when he finds out what she means to me. She's unlikely to survive, no matter what she does.

I need to move fast. She's no idea that she's walking into a trap. She thinks kindness and compassion will keep her alive, but she's putting her own life in danger to save her sister. She should have let me set this up. I could have kept her safe.

Maybe I still can.

I get on the phone, telling Horace to refuel the chopper. I don't know where Ellie's going first, but I can track her down. She doesn't know there's a GPS tracking unit in the painting's frame.

I look at the little flashing red dot on the map on my cellphone. Hovering above the blue.

She's already on the water, heading for the mainland. I only need to watch and wait for her to go to the meeting. See where that red dot ends up.

Once Esposito is out in the open, that's when I pounce. The only question is, will I get there in time?

TWENTY-ONE

ELLIE

I get the boat across the open water to Gordon's Cove. It's not the sea that makes the journey difficult. There's no wind and the navigation system is easy enough to use.

It's the fact that every yard that takes me away from the island pulls at me. It's like I've one end of an elastic cord tied around my waist, the other end back at Marco's house. The further out I go, the more the cord is stretching, getting ready to yank me back off my feet any moment.

What I need is some kind of knife to cut through that cord. I can't go back there. I can't return to him, not now. I've lied. I told him I was happy to take his deal. Made him think everything was going ahead. Then I ran, took the painting first chance I got. Made him think I was looking at the books when the entire time I was preparing to take the painting.

I had to do it. It's the only way to save my sister. Marco goes in all guns blazing and she'll end up dead, I just know it. He's already made it all clear with his whole, 'no mercy, no compassion,' thing.

I climb out of the boat with the painting under my arm. This is it. I've made my decision. I'm not getting involved with Marco Alessi any longer. He's bad news. Big time. First, there's the fact he can kill two people out on the street, tell me to show less compassion. Then there's the fact that my entire body is trying to turn me around, go back to him, beg his forgiveness. I'm not his submissive. I will not become one.

I can't go back there.

I go into the parking garage. Or at least, I try to. Security has been amped up since I stole the Bentley. There are guards circling the place, guns on hips, radios ready to call in any sign of trouble. I make a swift turn and head up and out of there, making my way into town. I run my hands along parked car doors until I find one unlocked. It's a battered old Chevy with an engine that sounds nervous about getting moving. I know how it feels.

I make my way out of Gordon's Cove, taking several deep breaths. I can do this. All I have to do is arrange the meeting with Esposito. I memorized the number. I can steal a cellphone. Mine's back on the island. Call Esposito, set up a meeting. I've got twenty-four hours to spare. Plenty of time to get back to the city.

Give him the painting, get my sister and get as far away from this state as it's possible to get. Move somewhere new, change our names, start again far away from these two rival Dons who will end up killing each other sooner or later.

That thought hits my gut like I've been punched. The thought of Marco dead. Gone without saying goodbye. I lied to him. Stole from him. Now I'm going to run away from the man I might love and I'll never contact him again.

Another thought occurs to me a moment later. Maybe I can go back to him. Maybe, once this is all over, I can have a proper conversation with him. Work out what this thing is that's between us.

No, I can't do that. How would that work? Sorry I gave the painting to your biggest rival. Did it for the lols? I've no doubt if he sees me again, he'll kill me. He said have no mercy on your enemies and I made myself his enemy.

I hate myself for doing it but this is family. I have to do it. I couldn't trust him. There's no way of knowing if he'd let me off the island in time for the meeting and if he didn't, Chrissie gets killed. I can't risk it.

Can I trust Esposito any better? What if he does decide to keep us both and the painting?

That's a pointless question. What choice do I have? I've burned my bridges with Marco. He's not coming along to help. He doesn't even know where I am. He's probably still searching the house for me. I'm alone. All I've got is my wits. They've kept me alive so far. Got me off an island where a mafia Don was keeping me captive. They'll keep me alive through the rest of this. Hopefully.

I get to the outskirts of the city before making the call. I think about going back to my place, but I don't think that's a good idea. Marco probably has people watching it. At least this car is anonymous. I blend into the other beat up vehicles around here. I stop by a convenience store and ask if he's got a phone. There's one in the back so I thank him and then go and dial Esposito.

It rings once, twice, and then I'm starting to think he won't answer. A third ring. What do I do if he doesn't pick up? I've no idea where he is. I'm panicking when the line suddenly connects. "Esposito?" I say down the line.

"Ellie," he replies, sounding as oily as ever. "How can I help you this evening?"

"I have the painting."

He takes in a breath. "The genuine article?"

"Yep."

"Good. Then you should come to me."

"No chance. You come meet me."

"I am afraid I must insist."

"Then you don't get the painting."

He laughs. The sound chills my blood. "You would give up your own flesh and blood so easily?" There's a pause and then I hear a shrill scream. It's Chrissie. I know her voice. "Stop it!" she's crying out before screaming again.

"Hear that?" Esposito says. "She'll lose another finger if you make another demand. Come to the old shopping mall at the end of Seventeenth. The east entrance. I'll be waiting."

The line goes dead. I wait for my heart rate to slow down before I set off. My hands are shaking too much to drive. He's hurt my sister. I want Marco's help. I want Esposito dead for hurting Christine. I don't want any mercy shown. He's hurt my family. The only family I have. I want him burned.

TWENTY-TWO

ELLIE

It takes an hour to get to the shopping mall. Traffic's heavy despite how late it is. I manage to find a space to park nearby but I've got to walk the rest of the way.

The mall is set back in an overgrown parking lot. The lot is edged by a broken chain-link fence. There's a sign at the corner of the lot. Condos coming here. Sign up for updates.

I remember hanging out here when I was little. It was one more place for me and Chrissie to keep warm. We lifted a fair few wallets and purses back then. It's funny what your memory holds onto. I have a clear image of where all the fire exits are in the place, the best ways out without getting caught by security. Can't remember the name of that store we used to go to but I can remember the exits.

I find the east entrance easily enough. I climb through a hole in the fence, cross through the overgrown grass that's covering the asphalt, and then walk into the building.

It's dark in here. Pitch black. There's a light in the

distance, so I head toward it. I wish I had my cellphone with me. I could have used the flashlight on it.

The light is getting brighter. It's one of those emergency ones, a sickly shade of green. It's lighting up one corridor, the one that leads to the center of the mall. I remember that part. A pond and fountain by the escalators. Little garden. Those rides kids like to sit on.

None of it's there anymore. I walk along the corridor and come out into the open space. The plants in the garden are all dead. The pond is dried up. The skylights smashed above me.

The lights are on in a store the other side of the pond. I walk that way. It's the only store with windows still intact. The others have all been broken by vandals long ago. Why's this one been left alone?

I get the answer a minute later. The glass is toughened. It's been beefed up since the place closed. I think I get it. Esposito is using it for some purpose. Maybe meetings. Maybe storage. Was it his name on that *Condos coming soon* sign? I didn't see it but I've no doubt he owns bits of the city. Some asshole always owns places like this. It suits him, old, rotted, past its prime. I only hope he's about to be erased same as this place.

I push open the door to the store. Inside the shelves are empty. It was a toy store. There's a couple of broken dolls and teddy bears scattered on the floor. "This way," a voice calls out. It's Esposito.

I walk to the back of the store. Sitting by the register is the man himself. Next to him is a curtain that presumably leads into the storeroom at the back. He's got his feet up on the counter and is flicking through a nudie magazine.

He glances up at me and smiles. "You brought the painting I see." He goes for his hip and I'm certain he's going to bring out a gun but instead he brings up a flask. "Care for a drink?"

"No thanks. Where's Chrissie?"

"Right back there, aren't you, my dear?"

A muffled cry comes back out to me. My heart almost bursts to hear it. "What have you done to her?"

"Nothing, yet. Give me the painting, Ellie."

He takes a swig from the flask as I take a step forward. "You promise me you'll swap her for this."

"You have my word." He puts a hand on his heart. "Come on, I tire of this."

I take a look at the painting. I want more than anything to go back in time. Take Marco's deal. Something about this entire situation smells wrong, but I can't work out what. I take a deep breath. Too late to change anything now.

I place the painting on the counter. Out of nowhere there's a knife in Esposito's hand. He slices delicately into the oils, lifting a segment. He smiles as he does so. "You did good," he says, putting the knife away. "Your sister always said you'd be able to do it. Didn't you, Chrissie?"

The curtain slides back and Christine walks out, clapping her hands slowly together. "Well done, Ellie," she says, nodding my way. "I knew you could do it."

"Come on," I say, running over to her and grabbing her hand. "Let's get out of here."

She doesn't move. "Go? Why would I go?" I look down at her hand. There are no fingers missing.

"What? Come on, we need to leave right now."

She shakes her head and starts laughing. Esposito joins in, tears rolling down his cheeks. "She still doesn't get it, does she?" he says.

"Get what?" I ask. "What is there to get?"

"Oh, this is priceless." His shoulders are shaking, he's laughing so hard.

"So smart and so dumb at the same time," Chrissie says. "That's been you all your life, Ellie."

She peels my fingers from her wrist, going over to the painting and running her hand along the frame. "What's going on?" I ask her. "What are you doing, Chrissie? Let's go!"

"You see," she says, turning to look at me. "We knew you'd never go get the painting if I just asked you. Not with your whole going straight bullshit. So what we needed was a good enough reason. Motivation, Ellie. That's what you needed, and I gave it to you."

"What are you talking about?"

"You still don't get it, do you? We wanted the painting, and you're the best cat burglar in the city. Proved it tonight. Walked right into Marco Alessi's mansion and brought this back without getting a scratch on you. He'll be spitting fire when he finds out."

That sets Esposito off laughing again. "Spitting fire is right. The dumb son of a bitch."

"You set me up?" I ask Chrissie. "But I heard you screaming. He was torturing you."

"Screaming like this?" She throws her head back and lets out a shrill cry. "Ow, Don Esposito, please don't hurt me." The scream turns into a laugh. "Didn't think I could act, did you? Don't act all high and mighty, Ellie. You're no better than I am. We're thieves. We're liars. We do what we need to in order to survive."

"You needed this to survive?"

"I needed this because that account number drains Marco Alessi's secret offshore accounts. Horace told us all about it. Surprising how easy it is to buy loyalty."

"Horace? Marco's cleaner? He told you about the painting?"

"Made a deal with us. He comes into Esposito's protection, gets fifty percent of the contents of that account. What he doesn't know is we're going to kill him and take the lot."

"No, you're not."

She frowns. "And why not?"

"Because I'll tell him."

"How will you do that?"

A shadow falls over me. I turn and there are three men behind me, all of them armed, guns pointing my way. I turn back to Chrissie, my heart sinking.

"Darling Lorenzo did the hard work," Chrissie says. "Got the crew together. Hired you. All I had to do was play my part and I like to think I did pretty well." She goes over to Esposito and kisses him on the cheek. "Didn't I, darling?"

"Of course you did," he replies.

"But what about Sergio?" I ask.

"What about him?"

"You were engaged to him."

"Was. He was just my ticket to meet the Don and here I am. We're going to get married, Ellie. You can be the maid of honor."

"Sergio's dead," I say, trying to get a reaction from her. I hate the way she keeps smiling so smugly at me. "Don't you care?"

She shrugs. "Makes things simpler. Won't have to put up with him whining about getting me back from the Don. That was why he went on this job, Ellie. I told him if he did well, I'd get back with him. Men. I swear they're so easy to manipulate."

"I hope you don't mean me," Esposito says.

"Of course not," she replies, stroking his cheek. "You're

my honey dumpling." She turns back to me. "We just have one problem that needs resolving."

"What?"

"You, Ellie. You are a loose end. We can't have that. I told Lorenzo here that we shouldn't kill you. Not with you being family and all. So we had to think hard, and we worked it out in the end. Want to know what we're going to do to you?"

"Let me leave here and never contact me again?"

She barks out a laugh. "Good one. No, not that. We thought it might be fun to put you in one of Lorenzo's brothels. You might enjoy it, you know. Finally, get some action. Also means you'll start earning your keep for once. Stop leeching off me. Time to stand up on your own two feet, Ellie. Or should I say lay back and open your legs."

I lunge for the painting, but the men behind me were waiting for me to make a move. They grab hold of me and start dragging me backward. "Don't worry," Chrissie shouts after me. "I'll come visit you soon, I promise. Bring some cream with me. You'll probably be pretty sore by then."

I'm taken out of the mall and bundled into the back of a van. A bag goes over my head as the engine starts and then I'm being driven out into the streets of the city. The men sitting by me say nothing, but I can tell their guns are pointing at me. My hands are bound as we roll along.

My heart sinks and I want to cry, but nothing comes. So I just sit there and wait. What else am I supposed to do?

TWENTY-THREE

MARCO

The GPS tracker hasn't moved for some time. Looks like the meeting is ongoing.

I'm coming in to land in the chopper. According to Horace, the location is an abandoned shopping mall owned by Esposito through a holding company in the Caymans.

Horace is on his phone while I'm busy flying. I bring us down in the parking lot. It's empty. No one in sight. "Stay by the chopper," I tell Horace as I undo my safety belt.

"You brought me for back up until the crew can get here." He pulls a gun out of his pocket. "You need me."

"I need you to keep an eye out here. Watch the entrance. If you see me running, be ready."

He nods. "Got it, boss."

Horace is getting too old for this, but Ben's still dealing with the bodies I left at the library and the crew can't move as fast as the helicopter. They're on the way but until they get here it's just me and Horace.

He's better out here. That way he can warn me if he

sees anyone coming in. I'm not going to be long, anyway. Go in, get Ellie. Get out. Clinical. No heroics. Move fast. If Esposito's there, I'll kill him. If not, I'll deal with him later.

The priority is to get her somewhere safe. I'm worried about why the GPS hasn't moved for so long. I'm hoping she's not already dead. If she is, I'll burn Esposito's businesses to the ground, destroy everything of his, annihilate his entire crew.

I duck through the entrance. It's pitch black inside. I use the flashlight on my cellphone to guide me toward the tracker. I find it inside the only store with the windows still intact. The painting's there, but she's not.

It's sitting on the countertop by the register. I don't pick it up. I get a horrible feeling it's been rigged to blow if I move it. I turn and there's a flash and then a booming noise that makes my ears ring. Someone just fired a gun at me.

I drop behind the counter. I stay down, turning out the light, listening hard. I can hear breathing out there. It's labored. Only one person. Have I walked straight into a trap? Where are my soldiers?

I call Horace, but he doesn't pick up. I can hear the ringtone echoing down the corridor at me. He's inside somewhere. I told him to stay out by the chopper. I'm not happy. He could get killed.

I move to the end of the counter, hoping I can find my way out in the dark. Another shot fires, almost catching me in the face. "Marco!" a voice yells. It's Horace's voice. "Polo. You ever play that game? Marco. Polo. Come on, I say Marco. You say Polo."

I keep my mouth shut. I crawl to the other end of the counter and wait for my chance. I can hear his voice getting closer. He's walking this way. Just goes to show you can't trust anyone in this life. I need him to keep talking. That way I can line up my shot right.

"How long you been working for Esposito?" I call out.

"You were supposed to pick up the painting," he replies. Somewhere to the left. I peer out but a shot nearly takes my head off, grazing my cheek. The heat of it burns my skin but I can deal with that later. I need to deal with him first. "Painting was rigged with an electrical charge. All you had to do was pick it up. That way you'd have died without pain. I made him agree to that."

"Why'd you turn on the family? We've been good to you, Horace."

"Your father turned on me!"

"My father was good to you."

He starts taunting me, trying to bring me out. "I told Esposito about the GPS. He wanted an entire crew to take you out, wait for you here. I told him I wanted to see it happen. Ellie's getting fucked right now, Marco. Taken to one of his brothels. Taking all the cock in the world I bet, that little whore. Loving them all and begging for more."

I don't rise to it. I grip my gun tighter, biding my time.

"Do you know how many years I've wanted to do this, Marco?"

"Fucking asshole," I mutter under my breath. He's still getting nearer. I just need to wait for the right moment.

"Ever since the Don let you take over. He promised it to me, you little piece of shit. Told me I'd take over when he went. Any idea how much it hurt to see you in my place?"

I grip my gun tighter. Just a little further and I'll have him.

"So I waited patiently for you to get killed but you just had to keep on going. Like that battery bunny in the commercial, you wouldn't fucking stop."

I shift my position. Another few seconds and I'll fire.

"I know what you're thinking. You're thinking you can shoot me in the dark. I've got night vision goggles on and you've got nothing. Reckon you can make your shot tell?"

I slide backward, ducking through the curtain into the storeroom beyond. Horace is still out there talking. He hasn't seen me move. "I told Esposito when you brought the painting to the island, put it in the study. Told him everything. Told him how to get you out of your little hideyhole. Told you the boat was coming. Knew exactly when it was coming, didn't I? I've waited years for this, Marco. I shoot you and I take over your territory. Made a deal with Esposito. I give him your head and he gives me your territory."

I'm down on the ground, my chin resting on the stinking carpet. I've got the gun held out through the edge of the curtain. Horace is still talking to where I was. "If you'd picked up the painting, it would have been so much simpler." He goes quiet and then I feel the curtain moving. He's standing above me. "Goodbye, Marco."

His boot catches my gun and sends it out of my hand before I can react. I go for him at the same time as he fires. I grab his ankle and tug, sending him off balance. A bullet catches my shoulder, but it's only a graze. I can live with that.

He falls back against the counter, his hand touching the painting. At once the store is lit up. Electricity sparks through his body and his face turns into a rictus of agony. The jolt of power is even running through his night vision goggles, sending sparks flying.

The noise is bad, but the smell is worse. Charred flesh, acrid and sickly sweet. Whatever is powering the painting doesn't last long. When it dies down, it does so gradually. Horace is still gripping the painting as he slumps to the ground. The glow dies away, but there are flames starting to rise from the layer of dust on the shop floor. The whole place is going to go up soon.

Somehow he's still alive. His chest rises and falls in the light of the fire. The painting slips away from his hand. He looks through me, his eyes are glazing over.

"Where is she?" I ask.

He opens his mouth, but the only sound that comes out is a wet gurgle.

I grab hold of him, wincing at the heat that burns my fingers. "Where is she?"

"Kill me," he says, the sound thick as it bubbles up out of his throat. "It hurts so much. Please, kill me, Marco."

I take the gun he dropped and hold it to his head. "Tell me where she is and I'll make it quick."

"Fifteen, Harlequin," he replies. "Fuck, this hurts."

I think about leaving him to the flames. Then I think about what Ellie said. Compassion. Kindness.

No mercy?

I fire into his face, and then I grab the painting and run. The flames follow me. I get outside in time to find my crew on the way in. They crash into me and I almost shoot Ben before I realize it's him at the front of them. "Fifteen, Harlequin," I tell him. "Meet me there."

I run for the chopper, but Horace has sabotaged it. The rotors are screwed and the display is dead. I curse his name before yelling for Ben. "Need a car," I tell him. "Chopper's fucked. How many cars you got?"

"Three out on the roadside. You want one?"

"Keys."

He tosses a set my way. "Get someone to collect the chopper," I tell him.

"Larry can have a truck here in twenty minutes. You want it fixed or crushed?"

"Crush it. Want nothing that links us to the fire."

The place'll be an inferno soon, so Horace's body won't be identifiable. The shot took out his teeth so dental records will be no use.

I can't believe he would turn on the family like that. "What happened?" Ben asks as we reach the cars.

"Horace did a deal with Esposito. My body in exchange for my territory, working under him."

"Horace? Fuck, seriously? I trusted him, that son of a bitch."

"Me too."

"Now what?"

"Meet me at Fifteen, Harlequin." I climb into the front car and start the engine.

"That's one of Esposito's brothels, isn't it? What's there?"

"Ellie." I pull the door shut and race off into the night.

TWENTY-FOUR

ELLIE

I'm not bleeding anymore. That's at least something. I'm on the floor in a darkened room and I've no hope of getting out. I don't know how bad I look after my beating.

They didn't leave the light on when they left. There were two of them and they took it in turns. I'm in a basement. I know that much. It's a building being used by sex workers. I'm supposed to become one of them.

When they first brought me here, they tried to get me into one of the bedrooms but I fought harder than I'd ever fought in my life. In the end they gave up trying. It was sudden. They had got me into the hall by the reinforced front door. The bag was whipped off my head and I found myself facing the two of them.

They didn't have guns out, but they had fists and feet. Two men. Both tall, both overweight but with muscle under the fat. They introduced themselves. The one with the broken nose was Karl. The other one was Gunther. He had no hair except near his ears. Some kind of punk, I guessed. They told me if I didn't perform, they'd beat me.

They weren't kidding.

I fought until they gave up trying to get me into the bedroom. Instead, they brought me down here and I've been here ever since.

It's a bleak room. Bare damp concrete and some rotten cardboard boxes in the corner filled with 1970s nudie magazines. There's a camera pointing at me from above the door. It's the only light in here. A red blinking that never stops. When I move, it moves. I'm guessing it can see me in the dark. They can see me.

They're going to have to kill me. I've accepted that. I'm not getting out of here alive. There are no windows. The door that leads out of here is locked and reinforced. I've nothing to work the lock. The floor is concrete. No way of digging out. No drains. Nothing.

I've felt every inch of the place, limping my way around, waiting for the pain to subside. I've got chains around my ankles, bound to a ring set into the middle of the floor. The chains hurt my skin but the mental anguish is far worse than anything else. Even worse than the beating I endured.

They took turns beating me, trying to get me to agree to do this. Not happening. I'd rather die. I told them that. They told me there are fates worse than death.

I'm not in too much pain. I could tell they were pulling their punches. Don't want to damage the goods too much. They gave up after a couple of minutes and left me down here, told me I'd never leave the basement if I didn't do what they said.

I wish Marco was here. He'd save me. He'd protect me from them. Put bullets between their eyes and carry me back to the island. I was safe there. I was in his protection. I should never have left.

I made the choice to leave. I'm alone. He doesn't know where I am. I doubt he even cares.

I close my eyes and picture him wrapping his arms around me. I find myself crying. Silent tears run down my cheeks. It's the sheer unrelenting misery of it all. I'm going to die down here and no one will know. My own sister doesn't care about me. I've no family that does.

I think about Christine. I'm still struggling to wrap my head around the fact she set all this up. She knows what's happening to me right now, and she doesn't care. All she cares about is money. I can't believe she would do this.

I don't know how long I'm alone down there, but some time later there's a rattle in the lock. The door swings inward and the light switch on the stairs is flicked on. I shield my eyes from the dark, wincing as I try to make out the figure coming toward me.

"It didn't have to be like this," a woman's voice says. "You could have had it much nicer."

I blink again and I can make out Christine. She looks sympathetic, but I no longer trust her. I'm wary. Why is she here? She carries on talking, taking slow steps toward me.

"You could have it easy. It's not like it's a big deal. You have sex and you get paid. How is that any different to a relationship? You let the guy do his thing and he rewards you." She runs a hand along the necklace dangling down from her throat. "This cost my man half a million dollars," she says with a smile. "You could be in the same position."

"What position's that?" I ask. "Groveling at his feet or bent over on all fours?"

Her smile fades. "See how far that attitude takes you." She turns on her heels and heads back to the stairs.

"Why did you do it, Chrissie? Tell me that at least."

"You do what it takes to survive," she replies, crouching down in front of me, putting a hand on top of mine. "We always have. I'm just willing to go further than you."

"Used your sister to get rich? Is that it?"

"As if you wouldn't have done the same." She sneers at me. "You think you're all high and mighty because you won't fuck for money. Lorenzo Esposito is the most powerful man in the city and I'm in his bed every single night. He throws money at me, Ellie. It's wonderful."

"Then why do you even need the painting? Why not leave Marco alone?"

"Two reasons. One, Marco killed Elda and two children. Lorenzo, darling that he is, wouldn't let such injustice go unpunished."

"What's the second reason?"

She sighs. I glance past her at the door. If it wasn't for the chains on my ankles, I could make a run for it. As it is, I'm stuck here.

For now.

She sighs a second time, as if she's deciding whether to tell me. She glances behind her before whispering, "He's broke."

"What? You said he was rich."

"He was. The Feds RICOed his assets. We need what's in that Swiss account, Ellie. You could come in on this. I know I can get Lorenzo to agree. You can come and live with us. You'll like it, I promise."

"Be his concubine, you mean? His mistress? That sleazy motherfucker? You really think I'd debase myself like that."

She stands up, scowling down at me. "So you think I'm debasing myself? Go on, tell me what you really think, Ellie. Little miss High and Mighty. You always thought you were better than me, didn't you? Well you're chained up down here and you're going to be a whore for the rest of your life while I live the fucking high life."

"You're a whore too," I tell her as she grabs hold of the door. "You just don't want to admit it."

She turns back and smiles at me. "There's a client waiting upstairs. Arab sheik. Wants to do some real kinky shit according to his translator. Paid extra. You're going to let him do whatever the fuck he wants. Got it?"

"Go to hell."

"You'll get there first. You refuse to go up there, and my guys are under instructions to take you to the surgeon. Do you know what he does?"

I refuse to answer. I'm doing my best not to show my fear.

"He's a miracle worker. He can remove any limb without the patient bleeding out. Despite the drinking, he's a genius. Imagine trying to leave here without any legs, Ellie. You either accept this is happening or I'll make sure you lose your arms too. All on camera. Some of the clients like to watch that kind of thing. You'll be just a body, Ellie. You'll have the only parts you need but nothing else." She smiles at me. "You've got two minutes before they come and collect you. Think hard about what you want to happen next. It's going to be entirely up to you."

She slams the door shut and I sob into my arms. Fear rises up in me and I do my best to swallow it down. I need to think. If terror overwhelms me, I'm done for.

Think, Ellie. Think.

If they want me to go upstairs, they have to remove these chains. That gets me out of the basement. If they're sending me up to a room with a man in it, I have a chance. I can scope the room out, work out the best way to leave.

I'm a cat burglar. I will find a way out. I might have to distract the guy but I can do that. I'll just act like I'm interested for long enough to get the fuck out of here.

I don't know where I'm going to go. I don't even know where I am. I can work all that out later.

First, I have to get out of the basement. I need them to think I'm playing along, that I've accepted my fate.

I again think of Marco. I wish he was here. He'd deal with them all. Get me somewhere safe. I close my eyes and picture myself held in his arms. The feeling gives me strength. I can do this.

The door opens again, but it's not Chrissie this time. It's Karl and Gunther. "You ready," Karl says, waving a rope in my direction.

My heart sinks. I'm not going to get to walk up there. He comes over and wraps the rope around my wrists, tying it tightly in place. I flex the muscles in my arms, hoping to create enough slack to get loose the first chance I get.

They put a blindfold over my eyes and a gag in my mouth. I don't bother to fight it. I need them to get complacent, think I'm behaving. I feel the chains coming away from my ankles and then I'm lifted into the air. The two of them are carrying me, my legs tied together before we head up the stairs.

I'm trying to keep calm but it's not easy. The stairs seem to go on forever. I can hear noises coming from the rooms nearby. Grunts, moans, screams. I do my best to ignore them. I can't help them. I have to look after myself.

If I get out of here, I swear I'll come back and free those women.

A door opens and I'm dumped on a bed. "You sure you don't need your translator?" Karl asks.

A grunt in response.

"Right. Who needs it when you've got the language of love."

"All yours then," Gunther adds, slamming the door shut.

I'm laid on my back. The room stinks of sweat and stale coffee. I know someone else is in here. I can sense them looking at me.

I don't move. Not yet. There's the creak of a floorboard and then a hand strokes my cheek. I fight the urge to turn my head away. I've got to make him think I'm placid, docile, easy to ignore. He's standing in front of me. I know he is.

I wriggle my wrists. The gap I created by flexing my muscles is enough to get them loose. Is he watching me struggle?

I flip onto my side as if presenting my ass to him. As I move, I manage to get my hands out. He grabs my shoulder and turns me onto my back. I lash out, bringing my fist up to his face, hoping to catch him off guard.

He grabs my hand and holds onto it. "Keep still," he hisses.

My mind is racing as he reaches behind my head, undoing the gag. "Please," I tell him. "Just tell me what you want and I'll do it."

"That doesn't sound like the Ellie I know."

It's Marco. I'd know that voice anywhere. For a moment I think I'm imagining it but then the blindfold is pulled from my eyes. I look up and there he is, hidden under a white hood. He pulls it back off his face, putting a finger to his lips.

I try my best to sit up. He's already untying my ankles. "But how?" I whisper. "How did you find me?"

"Tell you later," he replies. "Did they hurt you?" He runs a finger along the cut on my forehead. I wince, and he looks furious. He glances down at the bruises on my legs. "I will kill them," he snarls, "for doing this to you." He puts his cell-phone to his ear. "Now," he says into it before hanging up.

He lifts me up to my feet, pulling off his white robe to reveal his customary black suit underneath.

There's a gunshot and then another, coming from downstairs.

"What was that?" I ask, grabbing hold of his hand.

"My crew," he replies. "We're sweeping this place clean. Come on. Let's move."

TWENTY-FIVE

MARCO

I take hold of her and hold her against me. She's rigid at first but then she sags, going limp and sobbing into my chest. "Thank you," she mutters. "For coming to get me."

I kiss the top of her head. "We need to move. Keep behind me." I kiss her lightly before squeezing her hands. "I promise no one will ever hurt you again."

She sniffs and wipes away her tears. I want to hold her in my arms forever but now is not the time. I cross to the door and pull out my gun. Taking a deep breath, I move out. Swinging the door open, I point the gun to the left. Footsteps, getting closer. A man appears at the end of the corridor. I heard him talking when I first arrived. Karl, his name is. He's running, looking back over his shoulder. My men are downstairs cleaning house. He's hoping to get away by coming up here.

He talked about how good a fuck she'd be. He had no idea it was me hiding under the hood of the robe. I knew the best way to get close to her was subterfuge. Had Ben act as my translator. Him and Lewis are down there right now. All they were waiting for was my signal.

Three men in the reception room. All armed. Me up here and who knows how many more in with the women. A four floor building that used to be a dive hotel. Now it's a dive brothel.

Not for much longer. When we go, we're burning the place.

Karl sees me and the gun. He skids to a halt, fumbling for his own weapon. I'm faster. I put one right between his eyes. He goes straight down. I stride over and grab the keys from his pocket. I toss them to Ellie. "Get the doors unlocked," I tell her. "Skeleton key. The one with the black tape around it."

She starts getting the doors open. Women come stumbling out, blinking in the light. They look pale, sickly, some of them half starved. "Get them out the fire exit," I tell her. "I've got people waiting outside."

I cross to the stairs and look down. Someone else is running up, pursued by Ben. It's Gunther. He was the other one with the big mouth, telling me how good Ellie would be, trying to increase the price. I handed over cash to him, more than he wanted, to make sure I was left alone with her. I didn't need long. Just enough time to make sure she's safe.

He steps out onto the landing, and I take my shot. Down he goes on top of Karl's body. I walk over and grab the wad of cash from his wallet. I pass it to the nearest woman before going to meet Ben on the stairs. "Place is clean," he says.

"The clients?"

"Dead or gone. Rooms are all busted open down here. Where's Ellie?"

"Safe. Where's the gas?"

"In the truck."

"Bring it up here."

I turn around and Ellie is helping a woman to the fire exit. The woman's only got one leg. She hops along and Ellie is talking to her as she cries, comforting her.

That's when it hits me that she was right. Compassion can be a good thing. Kindness can be good.

The two of them go out the fire escape. I don't want to let Ellie out of my sight, but it's not for long. Ben reappears with the jerry can and passes it to me. "Double check the rooms," I tell him. "Make sure we haven't missed anyone."

I start splashing gas into the carpet, pouring it down the stairs. Ben yells up to me as I work. "Lewis has been all through twice. We're ready to go."

"Good. Meet me in the van."

I walk over to the fire escape and look down. Ellie is halfway to the street, still helping the other woman. I spin around and tear off a strip of the peeling wallpaper. I bunch it up in my hand and then pull out my lighter. It ignites at once, and then I'm tossing the wad of flaming paper down onto the carpet.

It catches, and a wall of heat hits me as I turn and head down the fire escape. By the time I catch up with Ellie, the top floor is well ablaze.

I think how Esposito is going to feel when he finds out what happened here. He's going to be pissed. He's going to come for me. He's going to end up dead. I will finish this and then me and Ellie can be happy together. That's all I want. To make sure she's safe and happy. Nothing else matters anymore.

I get an arm around the woman she's helping and together we make our way down to the street. "Thank you," the woman says. "They took my leg." She bursts into fresh tears. "They did it on camera."

"It's over now," I tell her.

"What about the man who brought me here? What happens when he finds out we escaped?"

"I kill him."

The freed women are all sitting together in the back of the van, looking terrified but relieved at the same time. "Get them to hospital," I tell Lewis. "They all need checking over."

Ellie turns to me. "Thank you," she says.

I walk with her over to one of the waiting cars. I load her into the passenger seat. "Where are we going?" she asks. Behind us the fire is getting worse. People are stopping in the street to look up at the flames.

"Home," I tell her, getting into the driver's seat and setting off. "I'm taking you home."

TWENTY-SIX

MARCO

She sleeps like the dead. I'm not surprised. It's been a hell of a day. She stayed awake during the helicopter flight back to the island but she's asleep in my arms by the time I carry her into the house.

I put her in my bed and settle down next to her. I don't sleep yet. I'm thinking about what to do next. Esposito will find out what happened pretty quickly. He'll know I got Ellie back. He'll come for me somehow. I just don't know how.

The next morning I'm up first and down into the gym. I do my workout as usual, but it feels different. Knowing she's safe, everything feels different.

When I finish my shower I go back to her. She's just starting to stir. She sits bolt upright all of a sudden, her eyes wild. She starts gasping for air so I grab hold of her, press her to my body. "It's all right," I tell her. "It's over."

She cries into my chest, soaking my shirt. She doesn't say anything for a long time. As her tears fade away I kiss the top of her head. "Let's get you clean," I tell her, lifting her into my arms. I carry her through to the bathroom, running the tub while she sits and stares into the distance, still saying nothing.

Once the tub is full, I stand her up. She doesn't react when I take her clothes off her. She's covered in bruises. She stands still, staring into the distance. I pick her up and she doesn't respond. She only starts to come back to me as the heat of the water soaks into her limbs. I wash her gently, being careful to work around the bruises on her body.

I tilt her head back to wash her hair, letting the water fall to the floor. I don't care about that. I care about her. I rub shampoo into her scalp, avoiding the cut on her forehead. She starts to blink as if she's waking up from a dream, turning her neck to look at me. "How did I get here?" she asks.

"I brought you," I reply.

"Am I staying here?"

I nod. "For as long as you want."

She smiles and ducks down into the water, sighing loudly. "Good," she says, lifting her feet out and turning them in little circles in the air. "I'm glad."

I leave her to soak for a while, collecting some clean clothes for her. I pick out a pair of pants that aren't tight fitting. I don't want the bruises to hurt her. I choose a loose white top for the same reason. Plain underwear. I don't want her thinking I brought her back here for sex. She needs to rest. Nothing else.

"What's that?" she asks, pointing over at the examination table in the corner.

"You don't need to worry about that."

"Are those leg stirrups?" She turns to look at me, taking hold of the side of the bath. "What are they for?"

"For when you're done in the bath."

She gets to her feet, water and bubbles running down her body. "I'm done."

I pull the plug and then use a white towel to get her dry. I do my best to ignore the way her nipples have hardened in the cool air. I take her hand and help her out of the bath. "Climb onto there," I tell her, placing a towel on the table. She clambers onto it and lays on her back, her chest rising and falling.

"Now what?" she asks.

"I examine you."

"What for?"

"To see how well you are."

"Like doctors and nurses?"

"You can call it that if you want." I put a hand on the middle of her chest, palm downward. "Checking your heartbeat," I tell her.

"I understand. How is it?"

"Racing."

"I'm not surprised. I've never been examined while naked."

I lift her legs, bending her knees, placing her feet into the stirrups. "Going to shave you now," I tell her, turning and collecting what I need.

"Are you?" Her cheeks are turning pink. It's good to see the color coming back to her.

"Keep still." I apply lather to her pussy, doing my best to avoid plunging my fingers into her. That can wait. I take the razor and scrape it gently down her skin. Her breath catches in her throat as I move closer to her pussy.

I use my hand to move her folds from side to side, feeling wetness coming out of her the lower I move. I'm as careful as I can be, making sure not to catch her as I remove the last hairs from her skin.

Once I'm done, I rub her dry with a towel, apply moisturising cream, and then step back. "That's better," I tell her. "I can see everything now."

"We all done?" She bends her knees slightly further apart.

I'm surprised she wants to do this but I don't judge her. We all handle trauma differently. I get the feeling this is her way of reasserting herself, proving she has control and agency over what happened to her, that she isn't just a passive thing to be used and abused.

"Need to check your temperature," I tell her. "And a few other things." I pick up a thermometer and she opens her mouth. I shake my head. "Not there." I slide the thermometer into her wetness, easing it into her pussy, leaving it sticking out of her for a few seconds as the gauge moves in the right direction. "How hot am I?" she asks.

"Very," I reply. "Lift your hips for me."

She shifts in position and I press the thermometer to her ass, guiding it an inch inside there. Her breathing changes as I slide it back and forth a little, observing her reaction. "That's good," I tell her as I bring it free. "Tells me you're doing well."

I walk around the table and as I do, she reaches out, grabbing my cock through my pants. I bat her hand away. "I'm supposed to be examining you," I tell her.

"What if I want to examine you?"

I reach down and unzip my pants, pulling my cock free. "Open your mouth," I tell her.

She does as I ask. I walk over to the drawers by the window and slide them open. The selection isn't as big as in the other rooms but there are enough things to choose from. I bring out a dildo a little smaller than my cock. I walk back over, applying lube to it, my own cock swinging freely from the front of my pants, pointing toward her.

She's still got her mouth open. "Time for you to take your medicine," I tell her.

"Will it make me feel better?" she asks.

I smile down at her. "Definitely."

TWENTY-SEVEN

ELLIE

The next few days are the happiest of my life. If there's one thing Marco is good at, (and he's good at lots of things) it's distracting me.

He shows me everything on the island, giving me its history. Apparently it used to be a penal colony at one point, back in the later 1700s and early 1800s. Began life as a fort during the War of Independence. He points out the sections of the house from that time, the low walls in the grounds, the few remains of that era.

In the Victorian era the prison became a grand mansion for the governor of the state, a vacation home where he could observe the passing of the ships and get some much needed privacy.

That's what Marco likes most about the place. The fact he can relax here. Doesn't have to be on his guard all the time. Well, until I came along, I guess. He tells me he wants to move back to the city but it can't happen yet, not until Esposito has been dealt with.

That's his current priority. When he's not with me, he's

making calls, lots of calls. He spends hours in his study and during those times I occupy myself. I'm catching up with my correspondence course. Another good distraction from everything that's happened.

My bruises are healing, slowly. The cut on my forehead doesn't sting anymore. I'm unlikely to have any permanent scars. The mental scars will last though. Every now and then, normally late at night, the memories come back to me. Those are the times he's at his gentlest. He behaves like I never would have expected, comforting me, sitting up with me, holding me close. He helps me settle to sleep just by being himself. I feel so safe around him.

Since we first got here, we've only had sex once, on the examination table in the bathroom. It was everything I hoped it would be. He didn't spank me. He didn't tie me down. He was gentle with me. I loved him for that. I still do.

It's like he can read my mind. He knows exactly what I need. Right now I need him but he's still in the study. I'm sitting on a wrought-iron bench by the pond at the corner of the house, listening to the distant waves and trying to concentrate on my book. It's not easy. My mind wanders a lot. When I shut my eyes, I'm back in the basement. I was only there for a few hours but I doubt the experience will ever truly leave me.

Marco says pain becomes a part of you. He marks his pain with tattoos. Each one has a meaning, a connection to his past. Showed me an elaborate letter C for Charlotte. She was his first love, until Esposito had her killed. Told me the tattoo keeps her alive in his heart.

He thinks maybe I should get a tattoo. Maybe I will. Perhaps a butterfly flying out of a prison yard. That would be the one I'd get, if I was going to.

He comes to find me in the afternoon, and he looks

happy. "What's going on?" I ask him. "You're actually smiling."

He sits on the bench next to me. "You ever play chess?"

"I've played checkers a few times. Does that count for anything?"

"All right. You know in checkers when you make a move but you've only done it to force your opponent to make a move they don't want to but they have to?"

"You mean when they have to take a piece of yours but then you take a ton of theirs in a row?"

"Exactly."

"I need more information, Marco. Stop smiling and tell me what's going on."

He stretches his arms above his head. "I've had my people monitoring the Swiss account. Esposito turned up and tried to empty it in person. Took a flight all the way over to Geneva."

"Why not do it on the Internet?"

"Less traceable in person. Or so he thought."

"You seem remarkably calm about it all. Hasn't he stolen your money? Why aren't you more pissed off?"

"Because I had the account emptied except for a single dollar. That's what he's got out of me for all his efforts. A dollar."

I examine his face. He's almost laughing. "Hang on," I remind him. "I told you he was broke. Chrissie told me, remember. They need that money, she said."

"Exactly. That's my move. Emptying the account. He's only got one move left and he has to take it."

"What's that?"

"Come to get me. He'll bring a crew to the island. He knows I'm here. I've not tried to hide that."

"Yet you seem happy?"

"Ever see Skyfall? The James Bond movie?"

"Nope."

"What about Home Alone? You must have seen that."

"I've heard of it."

He rolls his eyes. "I can't believe you've never seen that movie. Come on, we are watching Home Alone right now."

"Yes, Sir."

He kisses me. "You'll understand what I'm going to do when you've seen it."

"Get lost before Christmas while your family are in Paris?"

"Not quite." He takes my hand and leads me inside. On the first floor, there's a cinema room near the back of the house. Inside are half a dozen armchairs and a long sofa at the front near the screen. "Popcorn?" he asks.

"Go on then."

He disappears. A few minutes later we're sitting together on the sofa. He's got an arm around me as the movie starts. Somehow I get drawn in. "How have you not seen this?" he asks during a quiet moment.

"Never got much chance to watch movies," I reply. "How have you watched it?"

"Child of the eighties."

"You are so old."

He turns and glares at me. "Watch the movie."

I dip my hand into the popcorn and nearly spit it out when Kevin slaps the aftershave on his face.

When the movie finishes, I turn and look at Marco. "So?" I say. "Why did I need to see that?"

"One, because it's a great movie. Be prepared to watch it in the run up to every Christmas. That and Planes, Trains, and Automobiles. Although that was more about Thanksgiving but a lot of people think it's a Christmas movie."

"Starting to see why you're single."

He throws his head back and laughs. "Might get a bit geeky about the cinema sometimes. Anyway, did you see all the traps Kevin set up in the house ready for the wet bandits?"

"Yes, I saw them."

"That's what I've been doing the last couple of days. Rigging the house. I'm prepped ready for when Esposito gets here."

"And when will he get here?"

"According to my source, he's on the way back to the States right now. No doubt he'll put a crew together as soon as he gets here and come in all guns blazing. Only I'll be waiting for him."

"Don't you need your people out here? Isn't it going to be a bit one sided otherwise?"

"I don't want him getting suspicious. I move a crew out here and he finds out, he might go into hiding somewhere. This way he's on my turf and he thinks my guard is down. It's the best way, trust me."

"But how can you be so sure he'll come out here?"

"He has to. It's the only move he can make."

"He could try to bring you into the city, couldn't he? Start attacking your businesses?"

His face turns dark.

"What?" I ask.

"I didn't think of that. Shit, what if he does the same thing Elda did?" He's talking more to himself than to me. "Fuck, I need to make sure he comes out here."

"Who's Elda?"

"Elda was his nephew." He pauses, wincing. It's the most pain I've seen in his eyes since he rescued me in the city. "He robbed a bank on my turf and on the way out, he shot two kids."

I frown. "Hang on, he shot two kids? Sergio told me you shot them."

He looks like I've punched him full force in the stomach. "I don't shoot children," he replies. "Elda shot them because they could identify him. They saw him take his mask off."

"That's awful."

"I know."

"So what happened to Elda? Where is he now?"

"I killed him."

"So if Esposito wants to goad you back into the city, you think he might shoot children?"

"I wouldn't put it past him. He'll be mightily pissed off now he knows stealing the painting was pointless. He's also lost his most profitable brothel. If he did get RICOed like your sister said, he'll be out for revenge and I doubt he cares how it gets it. Fuck, how do I make sure he comes out here and doesn't stay in the city?"

I think back to the books I've been reading. There's something itching at the back of my mind. I can't work out what it is. I rub my head, trying to make the thought come out. "What is it?" he asks. "You look like your head's about to burst."

"I've got an idea," I say with a smile. I explain it to him and at first he's shaking his head but by the time I'm done, he's nodding. "You sure about this?" he asks when I finish. "You'll be putting yourself in some real danger if we go ahead with your plan."

"It's worth it."

"If this works, your sister might end up dead. Can you live with that?"

I think for a moment. "If there's a chance to save her, we should take it, but not at risk to ourselves. We can hand her into the authorities, let them decide what to do with her."

"I don't know if they'd charge her with anything. Technically, there's no proof she's broken the law at all."

"But she handed me over to him. She set all this up."

"But she didn't carry any of it out herself. I say you let me shoot her first chance I get. No mercy, remember. Compassion is for the weak."

I look at him, and I see he means it. Maybe he's right. Maybe I should let her die after what she did to me. But she is my sister, the only family I have in the world.

I've no idea what to do but luckily the bell rings for dinner which gives me a chance to stop thinking about it for a while. Ben serves us both in the dining room. While I eat, he talks quietly to Marco in the corner for a while. I watch in silence.

Will my plan work? I've no idea but I reckon it's the best chance we've got. Marco comes back to me, sliding a brand new cellphone across the table. "Esposito just landed. Time to make the call."

I pick up the phone, take a deep breath, and then start to dial. This call will either resolve everything or get me and Marco killed. I can only hope I'm making the right decision. By tonight, we'll know whether I'm right or dead.

By the morning this entire situation will be resolved one way or another.

When I'm done, I hang up and pass the phone back to him. "Well?" he asks.

I nod. "It worked."

He grabs my hand. "You're so smart!"

I look up at him and he's got this expression on his face.

It's like the words fell out of his mouth and he wasn't expecting them to. "Do you mean that?" I ask.

He squeezes both my hands in his. "I mean it, Ellie. I have faith in you." He kisses my hands. "You're a lot cleverer than you seem to think you are."

I want to tell him I love him, but I can't do it. Somehow I feel it might be tempting fate. I'll tell him after this is over. If we're both still alive by then. We'll know soon enough.

TWENTY-EIGHT

ELLIE

I meet Christine at the front door. "Did you come alone?" I ask.

Chrissie nods. "You alone in there?"

I nod back. "Marco's in the city hunting for your boyfriend."

"Lorenzo is not my boyfriend."

"He's not?"

"He's my fiancé." She waves behind her and Esposito steps out of the shadows.

It's a little after ten at night. The last couple of hours have been the tensest I've ever experienced. All I wanted was to turn back the clock, do something different.

It has to be this way. It will work. Marco is sure. I should be too.

I'm having to take the lead. I don't like it. Before he left, he told me I could do it. His faith made me feel stronger. I can do this. If I can just stop my hands from shaking.

I let them both in and then lead them through to the nearest lounge. On the coffee table, I've laid out all the paperwork they need. "Shit," Chrissie says, flicking through the pages. "I swore this was a trick but you've really done it, you sneaky thing. I thought you were too woolly for this, but you've been playing the long game all this time, haven't you?"

I shrug. "Like you said, you do what you have to in this world."

Esposito scoops up the papers. "You better be telling the truth," he says, pointing a finger at me. "Else you're dead. I haven't forgotten what you did to my property on Harlequin."

I do my best to meet his gaze. I picture Marco behind me, telling me I can do this. "You keep your end of the bargain and I'll keep mine."

"I am a man of my word. You get fifty percent of what's in these accounts and in return you give me Marco Alessi's body."

"It's up in the attic right now."

Esposito is already on his feet, dropping the paperwork in his excitement. "Are you telling me he's already dead?"

"Go see for yourself."

Christine looks at me and nods approval. "I underestimated you, Ellie. You're a stone cold bitch. Maybe we can work together after all."

"No need to. There's enough money there for all of us to retire to the sun and never work again."

"I have no intention of leaving the city," Esposito says. "Not after I worked so long to bring it all under my control. Excuse me, ladies. I must see his body. Take me to him."

"Go see. It's up the ladder on the fourth floor."

He pulls a gun out of his pocket and points it lazily at me. "Much as I would like to trust your word, I must insist that you take me to him."

I walk out of the lounge, my heart sinking. I know what's going to happen. Once he sees what's in the attic, he's going to shoot me. Should I run? Is it too late to change my mind about the plan?

I walk up the stairs in front of the two of them. "You better not be lying to me," Esposito calls after me.

"You have all the details of his accounts. What good would it do to lie to you now?"

He doesn't reply. I walk up the next flight of stairs and the next. Each step is bringing this closer to a conclusion. Soon everything will be over.

I reach the ladder that leads up to the attic. "Up you go," I say, stepping back. "He's right up there."

"You first," Chrissie says. "And if this is a trick, I'll kill you myself." She grabs hold of me and bends my arm back at the wrist. I let out a scream of pain. "Remember when I used to do this to you when we were little? Told you I could break it any time unless you did as you were told. Never had to make it snap, did I? You always gave in." She bends my wrist back further and I feel myself going faint from the pain. "Tell us the truth. Is he dead up there?"

I shake my head. "All right," I cry out. "He's up there waiting for you."

Chrissie's grin broadens as she loosens her grip just a little. "I fucking knew it." She lowers her voice. "Where will he be?"

Esposito is on the phone, saying something in Italian down the line.

"What's he doing?" I ask.

"Calling for back up."

"You promised me you'd come alone."

"And you promised us Marco Alessi dead not alive."

186

My shoulders sag as I whisper to her, "He's in the far corner, hiding behind a couple of old suitcases."

"Is he armed?"

"He's waiting for my signal. Won't come out until I say the codeword."

"And what's the codeword?"

"McCallister."

"Up the fucking stairs and don't think about saying that word unless I tell you."

I climb the ladder, my heart sinking. This is not the way I wanted things to go. More people are coming to the house. I doubt I'm getting out of this alive. I can only pray fate is on my side.

I climb out into the attic. It's dark up there and there's no way of knowing who might be hiding in the darkness. "Which way?" Chrissie hisses in my ear.

I pick up the candlestick on the floor beside me. There's a lighter on a shelf by the trapdoor. I flick the ignitor, pressing the glowing flame to the candle's wick. "Over there," I whisper back, waving the candlestick that way. Over on the far side are several old cases. "Behind there," I whisper.

"Right," she says, turning to Esposito. "Over there."

He nods, whispering back. "Keep him looking this way. I'll circle behind him."

The attic is a huge open space. There are cases and boxes dotted about and Esposito has enough light from the trapdoor to make his way across to the east side nearest the roof.

He's in the darkness now, a shadow amongst shadows. He creeps around behind the cases while Chrissie shoves me forward with the barrel of her pistol.

"Keep moving," she says before calling out. "We've got

your girl, Marco. Come on out and let's talk about this. The house is surrounded, you're not getting out of here alive unless we let you. Come on, you want Ellie's brains splattered all over your attic?" All the time she's walking forward, shoving me toward the pile of cases. "Come on out, Marco."

There's movement by the cases. She leans around me and fires in that direction. There's a flash of blinding light followed by a scream as she yells in triumph. "Got you, you motherfucker," she says. I can barely hear her. My ears are ringing from the shot firing in such a confined space.

She walks around the cases, snatching the candlestick from me and pointing it down at the corpse on the ground. "No, no, no," she says, shaking her head. "Oh fuck, no."

I look down. It's Esposito. He pounced on an empty space at the same time that Chrissie fired. She's shot him in the chest. Blood is pouring from his body.

Chrissie turns and her face is a rictus snarl of sheer fury. "You," she spits. "This is all your fault."

She drops the candlestick and it lands in a pile of old cloths. They catch light at once. She doesn't care, raising the gun toward me. I wince as she goes to squeeze the trigger.

She hasn't seen Marco behind her. He's been standing in the shadows this entire time, not making a sound, not moving a muscle. As Chrissie raises the gun at me, the growing flames illuminate his face. He reaches out in one swift movement and grabs hold of Chrissie, yanking her off her feet. She slips in the spreading blood, the gun firing into the ceiling. "Run, Ellie," Marco yells at me as the fire starts to spread.

I can't move. I'm frozen to the spot. Chrissie is up and turning the gun toward him. He's slaps her gun from her hand and it flies off into the spreading fire.

Chrissie roars and runs at him, hands stretched out like

claws, aiming for his eyes. He gets hold of her and spins, hurling her away from him. She lands heavily over by one of the skylights.

He's already running toward her. I look through the flames, but there's no way of getting across to them. Smoke is billowing in the confined space, making me cough. I waft my hands in front of my face, clearing enough space to see Chrissie running at Marco again.

He ducks to one side, tripping her as she sprints toward him. She skids past, crashing straight into the skylight. The glass shatters and then there's a loud scream that fades as she skids down the tiles on the outside. The scream grows louder and I know what that means. An instant later it cuts out. She's hit the ground.

"Run, Ellie," Marco shouts from the other side of the fire. "Save yourself."

"I'm not leaving without you," I reply.

"There's no way through," he says. "Get out of here. Get to the boat."

I curse out loud. "There has to be a way out. Can't you fit through that skylight?"

"Too small."

"But there are other ones. You must be able to get one of them open."

"All locked. Just go. Please, don't die with me. Save yourself while you still can. You can do this."

"I can't leave you."

"Yes, you can. I love you, Ellie. Do this for me. Save yourself."

The beams above my head are glowing bright. Another few seconds and they'll be ablaze. It won't be long before the roof collapses entirely.

A thought occurs to me. I run over to the trapdoor and

clamber down the ladder. I'm glad to be out of the smoke, taking several gasping breaths. I can hear screams downstairs. The traps are working then. Not that it matters anymore.

No mercy. No compassion. This is my chance to get away. No one will come after me. Not now.

I sprint over to the end of the corridor. There's a window that leads outside, so I slide it open enough to squeeze through. I cling onto the windowsill on the other side, shifting my weight until I can climb up the stonework to the roof. I can feel the heat of the fire on the other side. I see the broken skylight Chrissie crashed through. That means he's near there. I lean in through it. "Come over to the corner," I shout. "Marco!"

There's no answer. Am I too late? Has he been overcome by smoke already?

It was such a good plan. Marco as Rochester's mad wife. Hiding in the attic and waiting for a chance to get revenge on her husband. A few tweaks of the story and we could have been happy together. Instead, Chrissie had to drop the candle and if I'm not quick, Marco's going to burn to death.

I get to the corner skylight, groping in my hair and hoping I can do this. I find a couple of bobby pins. Two in fact. I can only hope it'll be enough. I have to try.

The lock is on the right-hand side. Usually I'd be able to get one of these open in under a minute, but my hands are shaking. The wind is icy cold up this high. My back is heating up, my legs burning hot but my hands are frozen. I shake them and try again, inserting the bobby pins and telling myself I can do this.

Marco's hand appears, pressed against the inside of the glass. "What are you doing?" he yells. "The roof is going to give way, you need to get the fuck out of here."

"I love you," I shout down to him. "I'm not leaving you." I shake the top pin, shifting its position. My hands are still shaking and it almost snaps. I hold my breath, wincing as I pray for it to hold. It does, just.

I twist it again, finding the right point for the final tumbler. With a click, I know it's done and just in time. The roof is creaking, flames licking up through the tiles and getting closer with every passing second.

Marco shoves the window open and clambers out, grabbing me and kissing me. "You're an idiot," he says. "You could have been killed."

"So could you," I reply, kissing him back.

"Let's move," he says, running to the edge of the roof and staring down past the guttering. "Any ideas?"

"The pond," I shout. "How deep is it?"

"We'll soon find out," he replies. I take a deep breath and go to jump but my feet won't move. Behind me there's a roar as a beam collapses into the attic. Flames rise up into the night along with a thick black cloud of smoke. "You can do this," he says. "I believe in you."

"Fuck it," I reply and leap off the edge. For a moment I don't weigh anything. I'm floating in the air. Then gravity catches me and I accelerate downward. I see the ground coming up to meet me and then I'm plunging into the pond.

It's deeper than I thought but the bottom is still hurtling upward too fast. I hit it and plunge into silt and mud, the thickness cushioning my fall, preventing any broken limbs. I look to my left and Marco flies past me, landing heavier. He lets out a cry of pain as bubbles fly up to the surface.

We both kick out, swimming upward and pulling ourselves onto the ground. I take a deep gasping breath, the heat of the fire warming my skin as I roll away from the house. Marco crawls after me, grimacing as he moves. "You all right?" he asks. "You alive?"

"Just about," I reply. I can't move any further. I collapse to the ground, rolling onto my back and looking up at the house. "Your home," I say. "I'm so sorry, Marco."

He is sitting next to me and I can tell his right ankle's broken. "It's all right," he replies. "I was thinking it was maybe time to move back to my city place." He lays back, his face turning pale.

"How bad is it?" I ask as he rubs his leg.

"I'll be all right."

"Your ankle seems to be sideways, Marco."

He shrugs. "I can handle pain." He grunts as he tries and fails to get up. I get an arm around him and somehow we get to our feet. He leans on me and it's heavy going, but we gradually make it to the boat.

Once we're onboard, he collapses onto his back, his face whiter than ever. "Stay there and don't move," I tell him. "I'll get you to hospital."

"Ellie," he says, lifting his neck to look at me.

"What?"

"Your plan worked. Told you it would."

I look back at the house, which is a raging inferno. "Doesn't feel like a complete success," I say.

"I'm sorry about your sister," he replies.

I say nothing else. I take the controls and get us motoring out of the harbor into open water, leaving the island, and the fire, far behind us.

TWENTY-NINE

MARCO

O nce we're out of the hospital, we go to my city place. We take the elevator to the penthouse. "You own all of this?" she asks, looking out through the glass doors as the floors flash by.

"I do," I reply, leaning back against the wall behind me. It's good to take the weight off my leg. It's wrapped in plaster and they gave me a crutch in the emergency room. Patched up my shoulder too.

I'll have to make do with a limp but it was worth it. We're both alive. Esposito is dead. Christine too. It's over. I don't care how long it takes for the broken bone to mend. I've got plenty of time. No more running around. Time to settle down and start a family.

"Do you need to live in a building this big?"

"I don't live in the whole thing. Just the penthouse."

The doors open and we step out into the entrance hall of my city place. The air is a little stale. It's been a while since I've been here. Soon have that aired out. I'm going to be spending a lot of time here now.

"What do you think?" I ask once we're inside.

"It's fucking enormous," she replies, spinning around on the spot. "How could you afford this?"

"Business," I reply. That one word incorporates a lot of things. Some of it more legal than others. It's funny. In the last few years I've made more profits from legitimate enterprise than I ever have from crime. It's like Robert Wagner in Austin Powers, pointing out to Mr. Evil that Virtuacon made billions from real estate. I wonder sometimes if that's the same for all the families.

Not that it matters anymore. I'll be leaving my consigliere to run the day to day things. I've got other priorities now the war is over.

She takes a shower while I make coffee. I want to join her in there but I've got the place to get ready. I start pulling off dust covers while she hums to herself.

She comes out wearing one of my shirts and my cock is instantly hard. She crosses to the window and stares out. She looks sad all of a sudden, her shoulders sagging.

"What's wrong?" I ask, limping across to put an arm around her.

"Are we safe?" she asks, blinking up at me like the traffic signals far below.

"For now," I reply.

"What does that mean?"

"Esposito is gone but nature abhors a vacuum. Someone will try to take his place sooner or later."

"Can't you at least pretend it's all over?"

"It is for us. You could not be in a safer position. You're going to become a Don's wife."

She starts, looking at me with her lips pursed for a second. "Hang on. I don't remember agreeing to that."

"What I say goes, remember. You're my captive."

"I don't feel much like a captive anymore."

"What do you feel like?"

"Taking the rest of the dust covers off the furniture. It's like a mausoleum in here."

We go around and get the place more habitable together. I watch her tossing the dust covers into a pile in the corner.

I can't believe what she did for me. I have never been more certain I was going to die than in the attic on the island. The fire was only a few feet away. I could barely see through the smoke. The window was locked and shoulder barging it did nothing. It was too high up to get my boot to it and the glass was reinforced. I was sure I was going to die. She had a perfect chance to run. There was no chance of me going after her. Instead, she chose to save me.

Now I'm thinking about marriage and kids and it's all thanks to her.

"What's this?" she asks, running her hand over a record player in the corner. "Are you into music?"

"Depends what you call music."

She's looking through the record collection. "How about this?" she says, sliding out a Ray Charles album. "Care to dance?"

The needle hits the vinyl and music starts to drift lazily through the speaker system. She skips across to me and takes my hands. "I don't dance," I tell her.

"Then you'll learn," she replies with a smile. "Or you'll stand on my feet a lot."

We shuffle around the room, my arms around her. I look down at her and do my best to move with the rhythm. "You're doing great," she says, smiling up at me.

"Not easy with a busted leg."

"Gee, I forgot. Come and sit down." She pulls the dust

cover off a chair and then stops dead, looking down at it. She stares back at me. "What's this?"

"Want to find out?"

It's the twin of the chair back on the island. Clasps at the corners to hold a person down, hole cut in the seat, vibrator built into the front edge. "Maybe," she says, spying the bookcase in the corner. Her smile suddenly fades. "All those first editions," she suddenly shouts. "I can't believe they all burned up."

I lean down and whisper in her ear. "Can I tell you a secret?"

"What?"

"They were forgeries same as the painting." I cross over to the side of the room and whip a cover off the bookcase. "Keep the genuine things here."

"But you acted like they were real."

"And you acted like all you cared about was the painting."

She rolls her eyes. "That's why you told me I could write notes in the books. They weren't the real thing." She comes over to where I'm standing and finds the copy of Wuthering Heights. "Maybe you could read to me?" she asks. "When we go to bed I mean. That is, if I'm staying here. I'm not trying to presume anything. I mean I guessed maybe I was staying but-"

I put a finger to her lips. "I don't want you leaving my side for the rest of my life. Now put the book down. You need to sit on this chair. It's time for your punishment."

"Punishment? What for?"

"Because I told you to run from the mansion fire and you didn't. You could have been killed."

She shakes her head. "I couldn't leave you."

"Nonetheless, you disobeyed a command. I warned you what would happen if you did that."

I take her hand and start unbuttoning the shirt. She hasn't got a bra on underneath. Her tits spill out and I can't help but cup them, feeling her nipples stiffen under my touch. I rip the shirt open, tossing it away, leaving her naked.

I want her so much.

Business first, then pleasure, I remind myself.

I lead her over to the chair and sit her down on it. I tie her ankles in place before doing the same with her wrists. Now there's no way of her getting up until I'm ready. "You are my captive," I tell her, crossing to the cabinet that contains the butt plugs. "And you will take your punishment."

"I will, Sir," she replies, looking serious. A flash of a grin appears on her face before she swallows it down.

I lube a plug and then kneel down next to the chair. "I will let you come," I tell her. "If you agree to marry me."

"And if I don't?"

"You don't get to come and you have to marry me anyway."

"Then I guess I don't have much choice but to say yes."

"Glad you see it that way." I ease the plug between her buttocks, watching her expression change. I'm glad she said yes. I can't imagine being married to anyone else.

"You are my obsession," I tell her as I bury the plug inside her. "An obsession that became a captive. A captive that will become my good wife."

"I will be good," she replies with a wink. "Most of the time."

I open her legs, moving the vibrator so the tip of it is pressing against her clit. "You're going to come for me," I tell her, turning the toy on so it begins to buzz quietly. "You're not getting up from that chair until you do."

She shifts in place, moving her hips as best she can to adjust her position. As I watch her, I start to undress. Her eyes are fixed on me as she starts to moan, the sounds coming from the back of her throat making me want her all the more.

It takes a while to get my pants off over the cast but I manage it eventually. Once I'm naked, she's on the edge. I take hold of my cock, stroking it slowly, rubbing the shaft while staring between her legs. "Come for me," I tell her. "And when you come, tell me. Shout, I'm coming, Sir."

I turn up the speed on the vibrator and her moans get louder. She grinds her hips forward, her hands fighting the bonds, wanting to reach out for my cock. Not yet, I think.

Another few seconds pass and I'm still staring between her legs when she screams, "I'm coming, Sir! I'm coming." Her whole body shakes and I can't resist her any longer.

I stroke myself as fast as I can go, reaching my own orgasm while her climax is still rocking her body. I spurt over her face and chest, enjoying the sight of her looking so dirty.

"I'm marking you as mine," I tell her as I push my cock into her mouth. She licks the last drops from me as I continue talking. "You belong to me now. You are mine for the rest of our lives. I will protect you, love you, punish you when you're bad, reward you when you're good. Think you can handle all that?"

I slide my cock free and she takes a deep gasping breath. "Yes," she says with a grin. "On one condition."

"What's that?"

"You never get rid of this chair."

I resist laughing as I untie her. "Looks like you need

another shower," I say, looking at my cum running down her chest. "And this time, I will join you."

I take her hand and together we walk through to the bathroom to get clean. It won't be for long. I like her dirty. Same as me. My cat burglar. My obsession. My Ellie.

EPILOGUE

ELLIE

One year later...

I look at the ring on my finger and find myself on the verge of tears. That happens a lot when I think about how lucky I am. I'm married to the greatest guy in the world. Ever since that night we first met, he's been in the center of my world, whether I liked it or not.

Luckily, it all turned out all right.

The wedding was perfect. Okay, there wasn't anyone on my side except Mrs. Henry but I joined a big family. He seems to have hundreds of cousins, aunts, uncles, all of them there on the day. I was given more cash than I'd ever seen in my life. Apparently that's a tradition.

They all told me how beautiful I looked, how they never thought Marco would settle down.

The entire ceremony, I expected to wake up back on the streets. It had to be a dream. Nothing this good could happen to me. I didn't deserve it.

I'm getting used to it. To being happy. To being content. To not having to worry where my next meal is coming from.

I'm aware that isn't the same for everyone.

I've met even more members of his famiglia since then, made some good friends along the way. For a mafia organisation, they don't seem that different to anyone else in this world. Some happy couples. Some unhappy couples. Affairs, arguments, laughter. Babies. Deaths. It all goes on around us, same as it does everywhere else.

The Esposito famiglia has disappeared from the city. With the death of Lorenzo, the entire organization crumbled. Marco has taken over. First thing he did was fix up the block where I lived. Not for me to go back there but for the existing tenants.

I asked him if he was in danger of becoming a decent human being. Earned a paddling for that. I loved every second of it.

We work well together. Never thought that would be the case, but we do.

What matters most to me is us two. There hasn't been a day that's gone by since the marriage when I haven't wondered what life would have been like for me if I hadn't met him.

Did fate send me after that painting as punishment for something? I had to watch my sister betray me and then die, falling from that rooftop. I was held captive and threatened. I was nearly killed more than once.

Or was it all done for a different reason?

I put a hand on my growing bump. Was this always meant to happen? Was this the way I was going to end up becoming a mother?

I'm five months along and I'm still getting used to the idea. We've been married a year. In that time I've got used to a lot of things. Like the fact Marco has to take calls in the middle of the night sometimes. The way he might need to leave me for days at a time when there's important work to do. I don't mind. He always comes back.

That's what matters.

It isn't very often anyway. Most of the time it's just the two of us and that's when I'm at my happiest. When he's away is when I catch up on my course. I'm graduating this year and he's already started leaving brochures around for post grad stuff. Wants me to keep learning. I'm only too happy to oblige.

I'll finish the course just in time for the baby to arrive. We're having a boy, did I mention that? We haven't picked a name yet but there's plenty of time. All that matters to me is that he's happy and he has a roof over his head. I want his life to start better than mine.

I know it will. Marco is making sure of it.

I walk through to the nursery and find him painting the last of the wall. "I don't understand why you didn't get someone in to do it for you," I say as he comes down from the ladder.

"My child," he says. "I do this."

"All right, Mr. Caveman."

"Ugg," he says, slapping his chest which gets a load of paint on his overalls. "Ugg ugg."

"Does Mr. Caveman want dinner yet?"

"As long as I get to eat you for dessert." He reaches around me and squeezes my ass, his smile turning into a frown. "What's this?" he says, sliding his hand under my dress. "What did I tell you about this?"

"I had to put panties on, Marco. It was windy as hell out there. Did you want me flashing the entire city?" I'm lying. I've not even been out of the penthouse today.

"I gave you an instruction and you disobeyed. You know what that means."

I sink to my knees, putting my hands on top of my head. He walks out of the room, already unbuttoning his overalls. I know I'm going to be here for a while but I don't mind. When he comes back he'll make the wait worth it. He always makes it worth it. Punishment and then pleasure. That's our life now, every single day.

I don't know how long he's gone but by the time he comes back my knees are hurting. He says nothing, just grabs me and carries me into the punishment room. "Over," he says, pointing at the wooden horse.

It's been adjusted so it can work around my bump. I bend forwards, knowing what's coming. It's what always comes when I don't wear panties. It's why I deliberately left them in the drawer this morning.

He ties my hands in place so I can't move until he's done with me. His hand slaps down on my ass a second later. He spanks me the same way he always does, with affection and strength. I gasp with each blow, my nerves coming to life. I get half a dozen blows before he applies the cream that soothes the sting a little.

His finger traces a line down the valley of my buttocks, finding my asshole, applying lube to it. "Maybe I won't plug you this time," he says. "Maybe I'll just fuck you there instead."

"Please, Sir," I say, turning my head to look at him. "Please, fuck my ass."

He reaches into his pants, pulling out his cock. It looks as obscene as ever, sticking out like that while he's fully dressed. I love seeing him like this.

He strokes it as he walks over, running it down between my legs, teasing my pussy by dipping an inch inside. I groan

203

and by the time I've exhaled, he's already pushing the tip of his cock against my ass, finding the tight little hole that can barely fit him inside.

He nudges forward, and I wince at the initial sting of pain. Gradually I widen enough to fit him in as he keeps pushing his way deeper.

Once the tip of him is in me, he starts to glide deeper, moving slowly, stretching me, filling me completely with his length. "You like my cock in there?" he asks, slapping his hand on my buttocks a second later.

"I love it, Sir," I reply. "Please, come in there. I need it."

He reaches between my legs, attaching the vibe to my clit. It's a clever device, uses suction to stay in place. It's like having his lips around my clit, buzzing like mad on my clit, bringing me close to an orgasm in under a minute. The closer I get, the faster he moves, thrusting back and forth in my ass, filling me with his length while I can only let it happen.

"I'm going to come in your ass," he says a minute later, still ramming deep into me.

"Do it," I tell him. It's the only time he ever obeys my command.

I feel his cock twitching just as my own body tips past the point of no return. He slams into me and lets out a grunt of bliss. An instant later his shaft is twitching deep in my ass, filling me with hot wetness. My own orgasm hits at the same moment, spreading from my clit to every nerve ending in my body.

I'm still shaking with the contractions of it when he slides out of me, untying my wrists, lifting me to my feet. He kisses my hand and then my forehead. "My submissive wife," he says. "My captive."

"My husband," I reply. "My master."

We walk out of the punishment room together. I'll be feeling what he's just done to me for the rest of the day. You know what? I wouldn't want it any other way.

WANT an exclusive bonus chapter where Ellie decides to break the rules in the naughtiest way possible? Click here to download your free copy.

SIGN UP FOR ROSA'S MAILING LIST

Want a steamy bonus chapter where Marco punishes Ellie for breaking his rules? Click the link below to claim your free copy.

https://dl.bookfunnel.com/q3hj2vvg7r

ALSO BY ROSA MILANO

AUTHOR'S NOTE

Although based in a fictional world of crime and small-town life, I want my work to be as realistic as I can make it.

Gordon's Cove is a fictional location on the coast and Los Santos is further inland. The mafia families I reference are entirely made up.

Any mistakes regarding mafia or other terminology are mine. Thank you for reading and feel free to contact me with comments about this story at:

rosa@rosamilano.com

GLOSSARY OF MAFIA TERMS

- Administration - Top level management of a family, consisting of the Don, underboss, and consigliere
- Associate - Works for/with mafia but is not a made man
- Bagman - Collects or distributes illegally gained money
- Barone - Baron or landlord
- Boss - Alternate term for Don
- Bratva - Russian mafia
- Capo - Captain, leads a crew
- Capo dei capi - Boss of all bosses, a supremely powerful boss
- Captain - Capo
- Comare - (pronounced goomah/goomar) Mistress
- Confirm - To be made
- Connected guy - Associate

- Consigliere - Don's advisor/fixer, always consulted before decisions are made
- Crew - Group of soldiers under commands of a capo
- Cugine - Young soldier desperate to be made
- Don - Head of an individual mafia family, decides who gets whacked, who gets made
- Famiglia - Family
- Family - An organized criminal clan
- Goombah - Senior associate
- Hit - To murder
- hitting the mattresses - Going to war with a rival family
- Initiation - Becoming a made man
- Kick up - To pass a part of income to the next up in the chain of command
- Lam - To go into hiding
- Make your bones - Gain street cred by killing someone
- Made man - An associate initiated into the famiglia
- Message job - Shooting someone in such a way to send a message (such as through the mouth)
- Oath - Becoming inducted as a made man
- Omerta - A vow of silence, punishable by death if broken
- Outfit - Another term for family/clan
- Pass - A reprieve from being whacked
- Paying tribute - Giving the boss a cut of a deal
- Pinched - To get caught by the police
- Rat - Someone who snitches after being pinched
- RICO - (Racketeer Influenced and Corrupt

Organizations Act)- The legal act that allows harsher punishments if it can be proved the defendant is part of the mafia

- Shakedown - To extort money from someone or give them a scare
- Shy - The interest charged on loans by sharks
- Soldier - The initial level of made man
- Spring cleaning - Get rid of evidence
- The commission - The body of leading mafia members who settle disputes between the families
- Through the eye - A message job to say "We're watching you."
- Through the mouth - A message job to say "This guy's a rat."
- Underboss - Second in command to the Don
- Vig - The house's take in gambling or interest paid to a loan shark
- Whack - To murder
- Wiseguy - A made man